Lights, Camera, Action!

by Beth Cruise

ALADDIN PAPERBACKS

Aladdin Paperbacks
An imprint of Simon & Schuster
Children's Publishing Division
1230 Avenue of the Americas
New York, NY 10020

Manufactured in the United States of America
10 9 8 7 6 5 4 3 2 1
Library of Congress Cataloging-in-Publication Data
Cruise, Beth.
Lights, camera, action! / by Beth Cruise.
p. cm.
"Saved by the bell, the new class, 6."
Summary: Megan and Brian become involved in the lives of their favorite television stars when the cast of "LoveSchool" films an episode at Bayside High.
ISBN 0-689-71886-1
[1. Television—Production and direction—Fiction.
2. High schools—Fiction. 3. Schools—Fiction.] I. Title.
PZ7.C88827Li 1995
[Fic]—dc20   94-42589

To everyone who ever wanted
to be a star

Exciting fiction about the new class!

Megan Jones was totally bummed.

As she trudged up the front walk of Bayside High, all she wanted to do was go home and crawl back into bed. Her black hair was pulled into a simple ponytail, and she was wearing jeans and a silk tank top. She just hadn't had the time or energy that morning to get dressed up for school. Not with everything in her life going totally haywire.

Megan was hoping to talk to her friend Lindsay Warner before class. Lindsay was the most steadfast, dependable person in the world. She was also really smart and knew just what to do if something was wrong.

As she headed through the main doors of the

school, Megan decided to go straight to Lindsay's locker, before she even went to her own. She was so anxious to get there, she didn't look around at all. She was totally oblivious to the fact that something very weird was going on at Bayside High.

Megan got to Lindsay's locker and stopped short. Where was everybody? The whole gang usually met at this spot every morning. For the first time, Megan looked around. What the heck was going on?

The hall was crammed, but not with students. It looked like an alien spaceship had landed. Huge halogen lights on spindly black stands were set up all over the hallway, pointed at seemingly haphazard angles. Big aluminum umbrellas were in every corner, reflecting the light to other spots. And about a hundred guys wearing tool belts were running around shouting to one another.

"You can't stand there, miss," a gruff voice said behind her. Startled, Megan moved aside as one of the guys stepped past her, unrolling a large wire that was slung over his shoulder. She took a few steps backward, then bumped into somebody else.

"Whoops! Hey, little girlie, better get clear of the set," another guy said to her. He was busy putting black tape on the floor.

"Sorry," Megan apologized. *Is this the wrong high*

school? she wondered. *Or have I stepped into the Twilight Zone?*

"Megan!" She felt someone yank at her arm from behind, pulling her over to the other end of the hall. It was Lindsay.

"There you are!" Megan said, feeling a rush of relief at the sight of her friend. "What's going on?"

"Don't you remember?" Lindsay said. "They're filming part of the *LoveSchool* movie here this week!"

"Oh, right." Megan couldn't believe she had forgotten. *LoveSchool* was the hottest show on television every Wednesday night, and the only thing anyone could talk about on Thursday. Megan thought it was kind of stupid—too much like a soap opera, and with all kinds of crazy plot turns that didn't make sense. But people couldn't get enough of Courtenay Amour and Joe Rollins, the stars of the show. So the producers were making a TV movie based on the show.

Courtenay and Joe were boyfriend and girlfriend in real life. They were always on *Entertainment Tonight* and in magazines, holding hands and flashing brilliant Hollywood smiles at the camera. And they were going to spend a week at Bayside, shooting scenes for the film.

"Well, that's really great," Megan said, looking around at the mess all this was creating in the hallway. "How do I get to biology class?"

"I can't believe you!" Lindsay playfully whacked her with a notebook. "Aren't you excited?"

"Hey, you guys!" Rachel Meyers piped up next to them, opening her locker and gazing lovingly at her own reflection in the little mirror she had hanging there.

Rachel could have been a movie star herself if she wanted to. She was totally gorgeous, with long blond hair and big blue eyes. The trouble was, she knew it! Rachel was completely obsessed with her looks. She admired herself in every mirror she could find. And if she couldn't find a mirror, she'd gaze into a spoon or a pair of sunglasses. Plus, she was a total clotheshorse. If she were in charge of Bayside, each class would require a change of outfit.

"I just saw Courtenay Amour in back of the school. Someone was putting her makeup on for her!" Rachel sighed. "I wish I had my own personal makeup artist. It would be such a time-saver!"

"Wow! And did you see Joe Rollins?" Lindsay asked excitedly.

"No! Would I be standing here if that hunk-o-matic was anywhere to be found?" Rachel replied. She and Lindsay gave little dolphin squeals at the thought of actually seeing Joe Rollins.

"You guys are ridiculous!" Megan broke in. "What is so great about these people?"

"Well, they're famous!" Lindsay answered.

"And totally glamorous," Rachel added.

"Yeah, *and*?" Megan asked. "I don't think either of those things is any big deal."

"Uh-oh." Lindsay peered at her friend. "Somebody's having a bad morning. Want to talk about it?"

"Where do I start?" Megan groaned, leaning against a locker. "I'm supposed to be taking the SATs in a couple of weeks."

"The SATs!" Rachel squeaked. "Don't say those letters. They make me break out!" She examined her face anxiously, as if there would be an instant reaction to the mention of the college-admission test. Then she turned back to Megan, a quizzical look on her face. "Aren't you a couple of years early?"

"I want to take some advanced courses at the community college this summer. But I need the SATs to qualify for them, and the test is in two weeks."

"That's awful!" Lindsay said. "You must be really nervous!"

"That's not even half of it. I'm studying for the test on top of my regular schoolwork, so it's totally hectic, right? Well, I haven't had any time to train

5

Trouble. And I think he's trying to live up to his name!"

"But he's so cute!" Lindsay objected. It was true. Megan's puppy—which was quickly turning into a dog—had big, heart-melting brown eyes and giant feet. Even when he did something wrong, it was hard to get mad at that adorable face. He made Megan and her friends understand why people talked about puppy-dog eyes.

"He's cute when he wants to be," Megan admitted. "But yesterday he ran away again. I looked all over the neighborhood for him, but it was like looking for the Invisible Dog. I mean, he was gone!"

"Did you find him?" Lindsay asked anxiously.

"Of course I did." Megan sighed. "I finally went home, and there he was—dragging an entire rosebush across the backyard!"

"Wow, was your mom mad that he dug up her rose-bushes?" Rachel wondered.

"We don't *have* rosebushes," Megan groaned. "It was from someone else's yard!"

"Ooooh." Lindsay and Rachel nodded their heads in unison, finally understanding the extent of Trouble's troubles.

"I yelled at him, but he doesn't seem to understand. He just stares at me as if I'm some kind of crabby, bothersome human!"

"So the SATs and Trouble," Lindsay said. "Anything else going wrong?"

"My love life," Megan said. "With all this happening, I haven't had any time to see Dave."

Dave Williams was Megan's boyfriend. At least, he was supposed to be her boyfriend. . . . Megan had barely talked to him in the last week. Between his hectic study schedule and her ridiculous list of responsibilities, they were having an impossible time hooking up.

"So the last thing I have time to think about is *LoveSchool*," Megan finished, shaking her head. "I don't have time to watch a TV movie, let alone watch them film stuff for one."

"Well, you should get your priorities in order," Rachel said. "No matter how badly I have to wash my hair or do my nails, I can always find some time to watch Joe Rollins. I mean, with that curly dark hair and green eyes, he's a total stud!"

"Hey, thanks!" Bobby Wilson popped up out of nowhere and grinned happily. "I didn't know you noticed, Rachel, but I do try to take care of my appearance."

"I said *stud*, not *dud*, Bobby," Rachel replied, grimacing.

Bobby was unfazed. He was used to getting rejected, but his philosophy was simple: If at first you don't succeed, keep nagging. Someday, somehow, if he kept trying hard enough . . . someone was bound to respond to his flirtations. Anyway, these girls were his friends, and they were just kidding.

"I may be a dud," he said to Rachel, grinning slyly, "but at least I don't have spinach stuck between my front teeth." Rachel yelped with terror and went back to her locker mirror, looking for the nonexistent spinach. She scrubbed at her teeth with some dental floss.

"Here's *my* stud! Hey, Tommy." Lindsay kissed her boyfriend, who had arrived just behind Bobby with Brian Keller, the new student from Switzerland.

"Hey, gorgeous," Tommy said.

At first, people usually couldn't understand why Lindsay was dating Tommy DeLuca. Sure, they made a gorgeous couple—they both had dark-brown hair and dark eyes, so they looked like a perfectly matched set. But Tommy's favorite subject was auto mechanics, and Lindsay didn't know a Mercedes from a Yugo. Still, the old "opposites attract" rule was in full effect with those two. They didn't agree on much, but they were totally in love anyway.

8

Just then, the Bayside doors burst open and Joe Rollins and Courtenay Amour strode into the school. They were surrounded by assistants. One was still blow-drying Courtenay's waist-length blond hair. Another was attacking Joe's clothes with a tiny whisk broom. A journalist was shouting questions into Joe's ear and writing down his responses. And a tutor was shoving flash cards into Courtenay's face, trying to get her to memorize French vocabulary words. Courtenay and Joe stepped into a small spot that was marked by tape and surrounded by lights, while more assistants put tape on the floor around their feet.

"What are they doing?" Megan wondered aloud.

"They're marking where the actors are going to stand when they film the shot," Rachel told her, forgetting all about the fictional spinach in her teeth and gazing at Joe. Megan looked around at her friends. They were all transfixed.

"They don't even look real," Lindsay marveled. She was right. The two perfect-looking teenagers were like pictures from a book.

"Hey—quit staring so hard," Tommy teased her. "If you stare at the sun too long, you know, you might go blind!"

"Sorry, Tommy," Lindsay giggled, grinning at him.

"I only have eyes for you. But Joe Rollins is definitely a really close second."

"I guess Courtenay's pretty cute," Bobby piped up.

"Pretty cute!" Tommy said. "She's perfect!"

Lindsay whacked him.

"Almost perfect," Tommy corrected himself. "Of course, Lindsay's the perfectest."

"Ungrammatical, but sweet," Lindsay approved.

"Well, Courtenay's no Grizelda Finsecker," Bobby said, shaking his head. "Now, *she's* perfect."

"Grizelda Finsecker! That computer genius who transferred into my math class?" Megan wanted to know.

"You know her!" Bobby sighed. "I've got to get a date with her. She's like an angel!"

"I didn't know angels came with size-nine feet and braces," Brian said in his cute Swiss accent, his blue eyes sparkling. Ever since he'd started school at Bayside, he'd been trying to get a date with Rachel. He always turned the charm up extra high when she was around.

"I know Grizelda, too," Rachel said. "She's supposed to keep me from flunking my beginner computer class."

"What? You mean you actually speak to her?" Bobby was dumbfounded.

10

"Speak to her? I'm going to be practically living with her for the next week!" Rachel replied. "Ms. Fenster has really been on my back. If I don't pass the next exam, I'm going to fail the class!"

"She's your tutor? Oh, man. You have to introduce me!" Bobby insisted.

"Ugh, just look at her!" Megan interrupted, nodding toward Courtenay. She couldn't believe how much preening and primping was going on around the actress. "Does she do that all day?"

"Well, looking good is a big part of her job," Lindsay said with a shrug.

"I can't believe this! Are we supposed to look up to her? Is she supposed to be a role model?" Megan demanded.

Brian let his eyes drift over to the pretty television star, who was staring vacantly into space as the activity around her continued. *She is totally beautiful*, he thought. *Even prettier than Rachel!*

Brian was having a hard time accepting the fact that Rachel didn't seem to be interested in him. Usually girls couldn't resist his charm—especially American girls, who really liked his accent. But Rachel was different. She had a boyfriend who was a freshman in college. Luckily, the college was far away. Brian might not be a college guy . . . but he was right here at

Bayside, and that guy was a plane ride away! Brian had been working on Rachel pretty steadily, and he was beginning to think she might be responding.

But Courtenay . . . she was really something. Any guy who got a date with her would be known far and wide as a serious Casanova. The more Brian thought about it, the more convinced he became. If he could just be seen with Courtenay for one night, he'd have all the dates he wanted—Rachel included—and all the guys would respect him!

Then Brian snapped back to reality. There was no way he could get a date with Courtenay. Besides, Rachel was his goal!

"She's *my* role model," Rachel said. "I'd love to have her fashion sense."

"Whose fashion sense?" Brian asked innocently.

"Duh! Courtenay's fashion sense, Brian. You know, the TV star that just walked by?" Rachel looked at him as if he were crazy.

"Oh, I didn't even notice her," he said, grinning. "I was trying to figure out how you get your hair so shiny and bouncy."

"Wow, thanks," Rachel said, charmed. She flipped her hair over her shoulder. Then she gazed at the picture in her locker, right next to her mirror. It showed a heroic-looking football player leaping gracefully to catch a ball. "That's just what my boyfriend tells me."

The evil B word! It was Brian's least favorite part of English vocabulary.

"So, how is the big bruiser?" he asked, trying to sound casual.

"Well, I thought he was going to come home this week for his spring break," Rachel said sadly. "But he has some kind of fraternity function, so he can't make it."

Ding! A light went on in Brian's head. What a perfect opportunity! Rachel's loneliness could turn into his chance for a date with her. A major scheme started brewing and bubbling in his brain. It was crazy . . . but it just might work.

"What? He's leaving a great girl like you alone to be with a bunch of his buddies? I can't believe it!"

"It's true," Rachel said, shrugging. "It doesn't make sense to me, either. But he's not coming home."

"Well, I'll tell you what," he offered, putting his plan into action. "Since he can't be here, let me be your surrogate boyfriend for the week."

"My surrogate boyfriend?" Rachel narrowed her eyes.

"Yes! I'll be your special spring-break escort, instead of him. I'll do everything he's supposed to do for you, so you'll feel like he's around. Okay?"

"That's so sweet," Rachel said. She gave him a friendly kiss on the cheek. "I accept."

They all watched Courtenay and Joe finish setting up their shot and go back out the doors, still surrounded by people. Brian hardly noticed them, though. He was running through his scheme in his mind, trying to figure out if it could work. Could he start out as a surrogate boyfriend . . . and end up as her real boyfriend?

Brian smiled. He had a special sixth sense about girls. And he could just tell: Rachel was ready to be wooed. If he played his cards right, he just knew she'd fall for him. Soon.

And no one knew how to play cards like Brian Keller.

chapter

"**M**egan Jones, please report to Mr. Belding's office. Megan Jones, please report to the office."

Megan picked her way through Bayside's halls, worming her way around technicians, crazed makeup artists, and mazes of wires. Finally she arrived at Mr. Belding's office. The portly, balding principal was standing in the doorway. He was squinting at everyone that went past, framing the action between his fingers as if they formed a tiny movie screen.

"Uh . . . Mr. Belding?" Megan asked tentatively. "You wanted to see me?"

"Ah! Megan. Come on in!" Mr. Belding dropped his hands and ushered her into his office.

"You caught me," he said, settling into his big leather chair with an embarrassed smile.

"Caught you?" Megan was confused.

"You know," Mr. Belding said. Then he made the little movie screen with his fingers again. "Pretending to be a director."

"Oh, that." Megan rolled her eyes. *Is everybody obsessed with television and movies around here?* she wondered.

"Yep—I've always loved Hollywood," Mr. Belding announced, leaning back in his chair and staring off into space. "When I was a kid growing up in Palisades, I used to watch *The Lone Ranger* every week. I'd put a bandanna over my eyes and pretend it was his mask, and then run around yelling 'Hi-ho, Silver!'" He smiled at the memory. Then he rubbed his nose, as if it hurt. "Of course, I used to keep bonking into stuff, because I had that bandanna over my eyes." He paused, still staring into space. He looked lost in thought.

"Mr. Belding?" Megan said. "Was there some reason you wanted to see me?"

"Oh! Righty-o. I've got a big job, Megan, and I just know you're the person to do it!"

Another responsibility? Megan opened her mouth to protest, but Mr. Belding held up his hands.

"I know, I know. You're very busy these days. But

you're one of Bayside's star pupils, and you were the first one I thought of when Courtenay Amour's parents approached me." He leaned forward and whispered across the desk. "Courtenay needs a tutor!"

"A tutor?" Megan was totally flabbergasted. "But she has a million people following her around the set all the time. Just this morning I saw someone quizzing her about French vocabulary."

"Sure!" Mr. Belding nodded. "She has tutors. But whatever they've been teaching her, it's not sticking. Her parents thought that as long as they were here, in a *real* school, it would be a big help to Courtenay to have a *real* high school kid help her with her schoolwork."

"That's real nice," Megan smirked.

"And you were the first person I thought of! Aren't you thrilled?" Mr. Belding asked. *He* sure was.

"Mr. Belding, I—" Megan began, but he was so excited, he interrupted her right away.

"I mean, you're an honor student. You're absolutely responsible. And you're so mature, I'm certain that you'll be able to put aside your admiration for Courtenay and treat her just like anyone else."

"My *admiration*? Mr. Belding, I really think—" Megan wanted to tell Mr. Belding that she didn't admire Courtenay at all. In fact, she thought that

17

Courtenay was a complete ditz! But the principal interrupted her again.

"That is so thoughtful!" Mr. Belding beamed at her. "You want me to give the assignment to someone else because you're so considerate of your friends' feelings."

"Yes!" Megan nodded so hard, her head hurt. "That's it exactly. I feel it would be selfish to keep this job all to myself!" She hoped her quick-thinking little fib would keep Courtenay off her list of stuff she had no time to do.

"And that's just the kind of attitude that makes me trust you so much. I have total faith in you!" Mr. Belding looked genuinely moved. "Megan, you can have this job *all to yourself*. I wouldn't have it any other way!"

Megan slumped down in her chair. This was hopeless.

"Now, I don't think I need to tell you how much this means to me." Mr. Belding waggled a finger at her. "It's a real thrill for me to have *LoveSchool* filming here at Bayside, and I want everything to go smoothly."

"I know what you mean," Megan said weakly. "It's great when everything goes smoothly." *At least, I imagine it would be*, she thought. *I wouldn't know!*

"So your first meeting with Courtenay is scheduled for today after school. You should be at her trailer at three o'clock sharp," Mr. Belding concluded triumphantly.

"Today?" Megan sat bolt upright. She was supposed to finally spend some time with Dave after school!

"Don't worry!" Mr. Belding soothed her, patting her on the head. "I'm sure you'll be prepared to meet your role model by then!"

"Mr. Belding?" A young, busy-looking production assistant wearing a set of headphones burst into the office. Mr. Belding sat up and smiled. "How can I help you?" he asked.

"The director says we need a 'principal-type person' in the next shot, and I thought you could stand in for us."

Mr. Belding shot out of his chair, smoothed his hair, and sucked in his pudgy gut. He winked at Megan, giving her a thumbs-up sign.

"Hi-ho, Silver!" he said, beaming. "Don't forget, Megan. After school, at Courtenay's trailer!" He walked proudly out of his office as if he were stepping onstage to accept an Oscar.

I wish I could forget, Megan thought miserably.

o o o

"Listen, Screech. This is really important!" Brian begged.

"That's Mr. Vice Principal Screech," Screech corrected him.

"Okay! Mr. Vice Principal Screech," Brian said, rolling his eyes at Bobby.

They couldn't quite figure this guy out. He had graduated from Bayside a couple of years ago and was now a college student. As part of his college program studying school administration, he was supposed to help Mr. Belding run Bayside. But as far as Brian could see, Screech wasn't much help keeping the high school in order. In fact, he was usually the one causing mayhem!

Besides, Screech looked like a big kid with his mop of curly hair and his stiff, ill-fitting suit. And that bow tie! Who gave him fashion advice—Urkel?

"What was it you wanted me to do again?" Screech asked, stopping short. Brian bumped into him, then backed up a few steps.

"You've got to let me into Rachel's locker," Brian repeated slowly. This was the third time he had told him! This guy was totally scatterbrained.

"And I've got to get into Grizelda's locker!" Bobby piped up.

"I'm sorry, I can't do that," Screech said officiously. He held up a finger and recited, "'Lockers are the private domain of students.' That's from *How to Be an Effective Administrator*, by Seymour Verrinder."

"But Mr. Vice Principal Screech, this is in the name of romance," Brian begged.

"Romance?" Screech suddenly looked interested.

"Yes, romance," Brian said. "I'm desperately trying to get a date with this girl. Won't you help me?"

"Romance," Screech said, his eyes focused on something far away. He knew what it was like to be desperate about a girl. "That's beautiful."

"Think about it, Mr. Vice Principal Screech," Brian said, grabbing his opportunity. "I've been pining away for this girl. But she just won't notice me! Now I have a chance to find my way into her heart. You've got to help me!"

Screech sniffed. "That's exactly how I used to feel about Lisa."

"Lisa?" Bobby wondered.

"Yeah. Lisa Turtle. The most bee-you-tee-ful girl ever to grace the hallowed halls of Bayside." Screech gazed into space, lost in his memories. Then he suddenly shook himself and stood tall. He clapped Brian on the shoulder.

"All right, you lovelorn young man. I'll be your Cupid," he assured him. "Let's open those lockers!"

Forty-five minutes later, his lungs aching, Brian ran around the corner to watch Rachel's approach.

"Are you sure this is going to work?" Bobby asked.

"Believe me. It's foolproof."

Rachel was coming down the hall, heading toward her locker and carrying an armful of books. When she opened her locker, she gave a gasp of surprise. A rainbow-colored avalanche of tiny balloons spilled out of the locker, bouncing gently around her feet.

Just then Lindsay and Megan came down the hall. "Oh my gosh!" Lindsay said, looking at all the balloons. "This is so romantic!"

"Who did this?" Megan wanted to know.

"I don't know!" Rachel squinted into her locker. Then she reached in and pulled out a beautiful orange tiger lily.

"'All the colors of the rainbow pale in comparison to Rachel—from Brian,'" she read aloud from a card attached to the flower.

"Aaaaaawwwwww!" the three girls cried in unison. That was Brian's cue. He came striding out of his hiding place.

"Who did all this?" he asked innocently.

"Oh, Brian. This was so sweet," Rachel said, looking as if she were about to melt. "Thank you." She smiled at him from behind the bright flower.

"Hi, Rachel," Grizelda said, arriving at her locker across the hall. "Wow, nice balloons."

"Thanks. They were a gift from Brian!"

"That's so romantic!" Grizelda twirled the combination to her locker and opened the door. Then she let out a shriek as a series of loud pops filled the air.

"Hit the deck!" Screech bellowed, running down the hallway past them.

"What was that?" Rachel demanded, her hand over her heart.

"I don't know. It sounded like"—Grizelda opened her locker all the way, and looked inside—"balloons," she said mournfully.

Her locker was full of limp, sad-looking hunks of rubber. She reached in and pulled out a bouquet of roses.

"'Color my world, you rosy posy—from Bobby,'" she read aloud from the flowers' card.

Bobby looked like he wanted to sink through the floor. Grizelda gaped at him from behind her thick bifocals. She didn't look pleased.

"I wanted to give her roses," he whispered to Brian. "I thought they were the flowers of love."

"Well, before you go sticking flowers in with your balloons next time, you'd better remember," Brian said, patting him on the shoulder, "roses have *thorns*!"

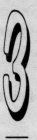

The football field behind Bayside had been totally transformed. Just for this week, it was the *LoveSchool* headquarters.

The neat, clipped grass was trampled and muddy. A dozen trailers were set up to accommodate the actors and production offices. And the staticky sound of walkie-talkies filled the air.

As Megan looked at the trailers, she noticed that one of them stood out. It was right smack on the fifty-yard line, painted pink, with a little air-conditioner poking out the window.

"That has got to be Courtenay's," Megan muttered as she walked up to the trailer and raised her fist to knock on the door. But suddenly an enormous blue chest blocked her way.

"I'm sorry, sweetie. Courtenay's not signing any autographs today," a huge security guard said. He had a black, scruffy beard and hairy knuckles, and looked like he could drop-kick the trailer to Pasadena. A tag on his barrel chest announced that his name was Tiny.

"I don't want her autograph," Megan answered, trying her best not to sound impatient. "I'm here to tutor her."

"Oh yeah? Well, let's just take a look, then." Tiny inspected a clipboard in his right hand. "Name?"

"Megan Jones."

He looked down the column of names, then back at Megan. "Sorry, you're not listed."

"Well, your list must be wrong," she told him. "My principal told me I had to be here this afternoon to help Courtenay with her schoolwork."

"Uh-huh. Just a second." Tiny lifted his walkie-talkie to his lips and started speaking into it.

"Stumpy? Tiny. Ya know anything about a tutor for Courtenay?"

"*Chhht.* I don't know nothin'. Have you seen Craft Service? *Chhht*," a fuzzy voice answered.

"No; let me know if you see them. I'm starved," Tiny said, laughing. He put the walkie-talkie back into its holster and shrugged at Megan.

"Yer outta luck, sweetie," he said. "Looks like today's not your day to meet Courtenay. I'll bet we could get you an autographed picture, though."

That was it. Megan had been trying to be pleasant, but Tiny's condescending tone was too much. She didn't even want to be here! "Listen, sweetie," Megan snapped hotly. "I don't want an autographed picture. I'm only doing this stupid tutoring assignment because my principal told me I had to!"

Megan was about to walk away in a huff when the door swung open and Courtenay appeared. She was wearing leggings and a T-shirt, and looked a lot less glamorous than usual.

"Tiny, I forgot to tell you about the stupid tutor they're sending," she announced. Then her eyes met Megan's. "Oh, hi."

Uh-oh. Did she hear what I just said? Megan wondered, feeling bad for about half a second. Then Courtenay's words sank in. *Stupid tutor? Who does she think she is?* Now Megan was really mad.

"Is this your tutor? Megan Jones?" Tiny asked.

"Megan Jones. That's her," Courtenay nodded.

Then she glanced at Megan. "Come on in," she sighed, sounding bored.

Megan stepped into the trailer. Even though it looked fancy outside, inside it was just a cramped little room. There was a huge mirror with lights around it, and the walls were crammed with framed pictures of Courtenay. Megan saw an ad for a diaper company, featuring an infant Courtenay with a big, gummy smile and wide blue eyes. There was another picture of Courtenay around kindergarten age, with her hair in tight Shirley Temple curls. And there were several large black-and-white head shots of her at various ages, pouting at the camera.

"My mom put those up," Courtenay said. "This one's mine." Megan peered at a snapshot of Courtenay and Joe at the beach, grinning.

"Uh-huh," Megan said. She put her books on the table and sat in a folding chair. Then she looked up again. It was kind of creepy, sitting in here with all those Courtenays looking at her. And they always wore the same fake, bright-eyed smile. Megan shivered. It was like being in some sort of weird shrine.

"Let's start with history," she said, opening the first book and trying to concentrate. "Have you covered the Civil War?"

"Is that the one with Denzel Washington?" Courtenay asked.

"What?" Megan was totally confused.

"And Morgan Freeman. You know, where they don't have any shoes."

Suddenly Megan figured out what Courtenay meant. "Are you talking about a movie about the Civil War?"

Courtenay's eyes brightened. "Yeah, did you see it? It was called *Glory*."

Megan sighed. "Courtenay, we're studying history, not movies. Now can we—"

The lesson was interrupted as a woman with frizzy hair burst into the trailer. "Courtenay! Babe!" she cackled. "Let's get workin' on those nails!" She noticed Megan and the books. "Aw, don't let me bother you," she said, sitting down, grabbing one of Courtenay's hands, and buffing wildly.

"Go ahead," Courtenay said, nodding at Megan. She didn't really seem to notice the woman squinting at her cuticles. "You were going to tell me about some war or something."

"Okay," Megan said. "Well, the North and the South were divided by their economic interests—"

The door opened again, and a small man with a crew cut bounced in. "Hey, Courtenay!" he said cheerily. "How's my girl?"

"I'm okay, Clive," Courtenay answered. "Will you take a look at my roots?"

"Eeewww, look at all the brownies," he said, pawing at her hair.

"Go easy on me." Courtenay smiled. "How was the heavy metal shoot you worked on?"

"Oh, you should have seen those guys," Clive whooped. "You know the lead singer of the Shrieking Morons? That Skank guy?"

"You mean Hank Sinbad?" Courtenay giggled.

"Yeah, him. Well, that boy is balding," Clive said, looking at Courtenay in the mirror. "I mean, receding hairline, bald spot, Hair Club For Men *balding*!"

Courtenay gasped. "But in the videos his hair is all over the place!"

"Why do you think he was wearing that baseball cap at the Grammys?" Clive sniffed. "Imagine what it'll do to his image!"

"*Anyway*," Megan interrupted. Clive and Courtenay looked up. "Should I go on?"

"Oh, right," Courtenay said, rolling her eyes. "Go on."

"Who's the schoolmarm?" Clive whispered.

"Tutor," Courtenay answered.

"As I was saying . . ." Megan was getting totally flustered. Her student wasn't even paying attention! But she had promised Mr. Belding, so she had to try.

"Western territories were getting populated and there was a lot of disagreement over whether they'd be slave states or free states. So the South—"

Again, the door opened. This time two people came in—a woman with a makeup box and another woman with a couple of outfits.

"Give me your face," the first one said.

"Whaddaya think?" the second one wanted to know, holding up a frilly pink dress.

"Ugh—they don't want me to wear that, do they?" Courtenay grimaced.

"Either that or this," the costumer said brightly, pulling out a slinky black minidress.

"Why would a kid wear either of those to school?" Courtenay demanded.

"I dunno. They just gave me these dresses."

The blond star let out an exasperated breath. "Did any of these people ever go to school?" she asked the air around her.

"Honey, *please*," the makeup artist said. "I'm trying to do your eyeliner!"

"Um, Courtenay?" Megan tried to get her attention. "Should I go on with the lesson?"

"I mean, look at this girl." She pointed to Megan. She's *really* in high school, and she just dresses like a regular schlumph."

A regular what?

"Maybe this isn't a good time to do the tutoring," Megan said, shutting her books.

"Well, that seems obvious," Courtenay replied haughtily.

"Okay." Megan was fuming. Didn't Courtenay care about anything but gossip and costumes? Did she think Megan was there for *fun*? "I'll go then," she said.

"All right; bye," Courtenay said casually. She didn't seem to care if Megan stayed or not. And she definitely didn't seem to care if Megan's feelings were hurt.

Megan stood up and walked to the door of the trailer. When she looked back, Courtenay was barely visible under the crowd of hair, makeup, and costume people.

"Bye," she said to the collection of people.

"Bye," a chorus of voices answered her.

Megan walked out of the trailer and slammed the flimsy door behind her. Then she looked at her watch.

Dave!

She had forgotten to tell him about having to tutor Courtenay. He was probably waiting at her locker . . . maybe they could still hang out for a little while!

She raced up to the building and headed for her locker. Sure enough, Dave was still there, sitting on the floor with his back leaning against the wall, his eyes glued to a book.

"Are you always studying?" she asked, scooting down so that she was sitting next to him.

He looked up. "Isn't that why you liked me in the first place?" he asked, grinning. "Where have you been?"

Megan groaned. "It's a long story," she said. "But I'm free for the rest of the afternoon!"

"But I only had a little while to hang out before my Chemistry Club meeting," Dave said. "And you're so late—I have to go!" He gave her a quick peck on the cheek and vanished up the stairs.

Megan sighed. This was so unfair! Aggravated, she walked out of the school and down the front steps.

"Hey, look, it's the Hollywood Tutor!" a voice greeted her. Megan looked around just as Lindsay and Rachel caught up with her.

"So? How was it? Was Courtenay totally cool?" Rachel wanted to know.

"Cool? More like ice-cold. She's a jerk!" Megan exclaimed.

"Whoa! Back up and start over, girl." Lindsay put her arm around Megan. "What happened?"

"First, the security guy didn't even want to let me into Courtenay's trailer. He acted like she was royalty or something! Then, Courtenay acted like an idiot. All she cares about is how she looks, and she doesn't know anything about the stuff we were supposed to be studying. And I missed my only chance to see Dave!" Megan felt better already, just getting all of this off her chest.

"Oh no." Lindsay was sympathetic. "I know what you mean. One time, Tommy was working on his aunt's Winnebago at the same time I was on the decorating committee for the homecoming dance. We didn't see each other for three weeks straight!"

"I remember that." Megan nodded. "You guys kept missing each other."

"Yeah, but we held it together," Lindsay assured her. "And it makes it even better when you do get to spend time with each other."

"Hmm." Megan thought about that one for a second. Then she looked at Rachel. "What do you think? I mean, your boyfriend's in college. Do you miss him all the time? Does it drive you crazy?"

"Well, actually . . ." Rachel blushed a little. "I mean . . . I was missing him a lot. But ever since Brian's been acting so cute, I've been thinking about him less and less."

"Oh my gosh, you mean Brian's love campaign is actually working?" Lindsay cried.

Rachel shrugged. "I don't know," she said. "It's just that I don't feel so lonely anymore. Brian is around all the time. And he's so cute!"

"See? He's *around*," Megan pointed out gloomily. Her situation seemed hopeless. "You and Brian get to spend time together."

"Well, maybe you and Dave will have a chance to spend time together soon," Lindsay offered. "Maybe you can both just check your schedules and set a time."

"Oh, sure," Megan said with a little snort. "We should be able to squeeze in a movie or something. Right after he finishes medical school!"

The next day, Brian loped up the steps to his Spanish class. It was his last class, and he was just in time. He was pretty psyched. He'd been working non-stop to impress Rachel, and his keen girl instincts were telling him that she was close to surrender.

Take the day before, for instance. Brian had over-heard Rachel telling Lindsay and Megan that she thought he was cute! And when he pretended to bump into them and offered to walk Rachel home, Rachel had actually *blushed*. As far as Brian was concerned, it was official: There was no woman who could with-stand the Keller charm.

He finally got to the top of the stairs and gave a long sigh. It was a beautiful day, and he wished he could spend it outside. But he was already late. Running a hand through his short blond hair, he turned and headed down the hall to his classroom.

Except the room was totally deserted! Where was everybody? Then he spotted the note taped to the door.

"ESTUDIANTES: CLASS MOVED TO ROOM 542," the note said. "This room needed for the *LoveSchool* movie."

Brian looked out the window. Sure enough, he could see the cameras and crew setting up for a shot, and this classroom was right in their line of vision. *I wonder why they wouldn't want a real classful of students to be in the background of their movie?* he thought, smiling. I guess we don't look typical enough. He was just about to go to the other classroom when something caught his eye.

Waist-length, thick blond hair. Piercing blue eyes. And a perfect body. Courtenay Amour was standing right outside the window, and Brian could see her perfectly.

Brian had seen her several times over the past few days, but she never ceased to amaze him. She was so glamorous, so beautiful. She was flawless. He watched her speak to the director, who gave her a pat on the shoulder. Then she walked away from the set, toward her trailer. And for some reason, her usual entourage was gone. There was no one near Courtenay except Joe Rollins. Brian narrowed his blue eyes. It would be so cool to get a really close look at her. And if he acted quickly, he just might.

As he passed the note on the door, he peeled it off and crumpled it up.

"Oops, the note fell down," he said. "I wonder what it said? I guess I can't go to class if I don't know where it is."

He raced outside and around the side of the school, toward the football field. Somehow, he managed to make it to the pink trailer before Courtenay. She showed up a half second later, with Joe. Brian slipped behind a rack of costumes under a tent and peeked out at them.

I don't see what's so great about that guy, Brian thought, watching the teen star follow his beloved Courtenay into her trailer. *Sure, he's good-looking. He has a great body. And he's a champion surfer. And he's rich. But he doesn't have . . . well . . .* Brian thought about it for a minute. He couldn't think of anything he had that Joe didn't.

Except the Keller charm!

And it didn't sound as if Joe was doing too well inside that trailer. Brian could hear Joe's and

37

Courtenay's raised voices as they yelled at each other. They were having a terrible fight!

"But I thought we were going to spend the whole afternoon together," Brian heard Joe protesting. "How can we go surfing if you have to be back here at three o'clock?"

"Well, what am I supposed to do?" Courtenay shouted back. "My parents have this stupid idea that I need extra tutoring, and that's when they scheduled it for."

"Well, unschedule it!" Joe insisted.

"*You* unschedule it!" Courtenay yelled.

The door banged open, and Joe came storming out. Brian ducked back further behind the costumes and kept listening.

"You don't care at all, do you?" Joe grumbled.

"What did you say?" Courtenay snapped from the open door.

"Nothing. Forget it," Joe answered, jamming his hands into the pockets of his jeans. Then he turned to face Courtenay, his dark hair falling into his eyes as he glared at her.

"It's just that I never see you!" he said. "We haven't spent any time together in so long, I can't even remember what color your eyes are!"

"Well, they're blue!" Courtenay shrieked. "All right? *Blue!*"

"Fine." Joe threw his hands up in the air. "Now I know. I guess I don't need to see you, then."

"I guess not," Courtenay said, folding her arms and looking hurt.

"Well, I'll go surfing with someone else," he said, avoiding her eyes.

"Do whatever you want; I don't care," she muttered. Then she went back into her trailer, slamming the door behind her. Joe stood there for a minute. Then he left, too.

What a woman! Brian thought, remembering the way Courtenay's eyes had flashed with anger. *If she were my girlfriend, I wouldn't let her get away so easily. . . .*

All of a sudden Brian was lost in a fantasy world. He saw himself in a black tuxedo with a paisley vest, escorting Courtenay out of a limousine and into a theater . . . standing back as she dealt with photographers and reporters. . . . Then she would turn to him and take his arm. "Oh, Brian," she would sigh. "Thank you for waiting so patiently. You are such a perfect boyfriend."

"And so are you," Brian would answer, leaning over and kissing her smooth, porcelain neck.

"Oh, Brian, you're so silly," she would laugh, her blue eyes shining. "I'm not the boyfriend. You are! Now, would you move your butt?"

Would you move your butt? Why would she say that?

"Excuse me. Would you please move your butt?" someone repeated. Brian snapped out of his reverie and realized he was still hidden behind the wardrobe rack. A frizzy-haired woman was glaring at him.

"Oops! Sorry," he apologized, moving out of her way. But he still had a big grin plastered across his face as he headed back to school. *A perfect boyfriend*, he thought. Then the wheels really began to turn in his head. *I'll bet I really would make her happy. I wonder if it could ever happen?*

o o o

"Half an hour!" Megan said angrily, looking at her watch.

There was no one else in the library to hear her. After finding out about her disastrous attempt to tutor Courtenay in the trailer the day before, Mr. Belding had arranged to try again. This time, they were supposed to meet somewhere more neutral, where the crew wouldn't distract Courtenay. Megan had a feeling it wouldn't make a difference, because Courtenay didn't seem interested in the stuff Megan had tried to tell her. And if someone didn't care about learning anything, the quietest library in the world wasn't going to make them study.

Anyway, she was getting pretty sick of sitting here. Especially when she could be studying for the SATs or seeing Dave or training Trouble. Why should she waste her afternoon waiting for an overgrown Barbie doll to show up?

She was just about to pack up her books and leave when the library door opened and Courtenay came breezing in.

Ugh, Megan thought. *She acts like she owns the place.*

"Hi," she said, trying to sound friendly.

"Hi." Courtenay didn't even apologize for being late! She just plopped herself down and sat there, staring at nothing.

"I was expecting you at three," Megan prompted.

"I'm here, aren't I? What more do you want?" Courtenay snapped.

"Right." Megan took a deep breath to calm herself. *This is a favor for Mr. Belding*, she reminded herself. "Well!" she said brightly. "I guess we'll get started. I thought I'd ask you some questions, to see how much you know. That way I'll have an idea about what to help you with."

"Whatever," Courtenay said.

"Okay. What war was ended with the signing of the Treaty of Versailles?" Megan asked, glancing sideways at Courtenay.

"I don't know." Courtenay sat back in her chair and gazed out the window.

"All right, something easier. Who was the New Deal president?" Megan asked.

Courtenay sighed. "I don't know."

Megan was getting totally aggravated. "What color was George Washington's white horse?"

Courtenay didn't answer.

"Courtenay? What color?" Megan prodded.

The TV star looked like she was a million miles away. "I don't know," she said again. "Blue?"

"Blue!" Megan sat straight up and glared at her tutee. "You're not even *listening* to me! How do you expect to learn anything?"

Courtenay finally looked at Megan. "Well, excuse me," she said snottily. "I guess I have more on my mind than you do."

"I doubt it," Megan replied, matching Courtenay's snottiness. "I mean, I may not spend as much time as you do thinking about my clothes and my hair. But there are other things to think about. I've got bigger dreams than finding the perfect perm!"

"Gosh, thanks for the life lesson," Courtenay sneered witheringly. "Except you forgot one thing."

"And what is that?" Megan wanted to know.

"I'm a huge star, and you're *nobody*," Courtenay hissed. "You *have* to learn all this stuff so you can make a living. But I've got it made! It's not going to make a bit of difference to me how the South won the Civil War or what the capital of Cincinnati is."

Megan was totally shocked. "The North won the Civil War," she responded slowly, enunciating her words as if Courtenay were a total moron. "And Cincinnati *is* the capital . . . of Ohio."

"Well, aren't you smart," Courtenay smirked. Then she stood up. "You know what? I don't have time for this nonsense," she said. "I've been working nonstop, and this is the first afternoon I've had off in two weeks. And I've got more important things to do than to spend it here."

"Oh, really? Like what?" Megan asked.

Courtenay suddenly looked a little deflated, as if she didn't actually have any plans. Then she stood up straight and flipped her hair back.

"I'm going shopping," she answered. And she turned and stalked out of the library.

Megan was left with her books—and her jaw—hanging open.

"Is that what's so important?" she said aloud, slamming her books shut angrily. "Shopping," she repeated, shaking her head. "What a *brat!*"

chapter

5

"**B**obby, what are we doing here?" Brian wanted
to know.

"Shh," Bobby hissed. "I don't want anyone to
see us."

That was fine with Brian. Bobby was a good
friend, and Brian was willing to help him out—but he
was such a weird kid! He was ducking in and out of
stores in the Palisades Mall, looking over his shoulder
and peering around corners as if the Terminator were
after him.

"Oh my gosh! *There she is!*" Bobby squeaked,
pulling Brian into a women's clothing store. He
clutched a mannequin, hiding behind it, then peered
out the window of the shop.

45

"Who? Who?" Brian wanted to see, too. Bobby grabbed Brian's arm and rushed into a dressing room. He pulled the curtain closed.

"Bobby, what is going on?" Brian was trying not to crack up completely.

Bobby just looked exasperated. "I told you before we got to the mall. Don't you remember?"

"I was in such a daze from seeing Courtenay, I don't remember much of anything," Brian admitted.

Bobby looked exasperated. "All right. Grizelda's birthday is tomorrow, and I want to get her something really special." He leaned in close to Brian's ear, whispering. "Megan says that Grizelda told her that she thinks I'm kind of cute! And I just know that if I get her an amazingly great birthday present, she'll go out with me."

"So we're here to get an amazingly great birthday present?" Brian asked.

"Righty-o, Einstein!" Bobby knocked on Brian's head. "The key to my happiness is out there, at that T-shirt store."

"The one where they take a picture of you and put it on a shirt?" Brian was baffled.

"Right again! I'm going to give her a picture of me, on a shirt. Great idea, right?"

"Sure, Bobby." Brian smiled at his friend. "It's a great idea, if you say so."

46

"The trouble is, I just saw Grizelda—here at the mall!" Bobby shook Brian's shoulders as if this were vital information. "So I've got to hurry over there, have them take my picture, and get out, lickety-split."

"Okay, guy. So what do you want me to do?" Brian asked.

"Go out there. Make sure the coast is clear. Then come back and give me the high sign!"

"The high sign?" This was an English expression that Brian hadn't heard.

"Yeah, the high sign. A signal, to let me know it's safe to go out there!"

"Oh! Okay. I'll go check." Brian strolled over to the front of the store, then stepped outside. He looked back and forth. No Grizelda. He went back to the dressing room.

"Okay, Bobby. The coast is clear!" He began to open the curtain.

"*Hey!*" a female voice admonished him as its owner yanked the curtain closed.

"Whoops!" Brian was totally embarrassed. He hadn't seen anything—just a well-manicured hand—but he *was* in the women's dressing rooms. He whirled around, looking for Bobby, and saw him scooting across the mall to the T-shirt place. "I guess my friend decided not to wait for the high sign."

"The what?" the girl's voice demanded. A hand still clutched at the curtain.

"The high sign. It's a signal that—never mind," Brian stammered. "He was hiding in here."

"Seems like a weird place to hide," the voice said.

"He's kind of a weird guy," Brian answered. "I'm sorry—I'll leave you alone in there." He backed up a few steps.

"Never mind," the voice said. "I'm not even trying anything on. I was just sitting in here, thinking."

"Well, if it's a weird place to hide, it's an even weirder place to think!" Brian said, laughing. The girl in the dressing room laughed, too. Then the hand loosened its grip on the curtain and it opened, revealing a dazzling display of waist-length blond hair.

The girl in the dressing room was Courtenay!

"Whoa," was the best reaction Brian could come up with.

"Whoa, yourself," she sniffled. "Haven't you ever seen a crying TV star before?"

Brian fidgeted for a second, not sure what to do. After all that sneaking around and watching Courtenay from afar, here he was face-to-face with her. And he couldn't think of anything to say.

Then he looked more closely. Courtenay dabbed at her nose with a little pink tissue and looked up at him.

48

Her eyes were red-rimmed, and a few renegade tears were rolling down her cheeks. Star or no star, this was a girl who needed a pal. He ducked into the dressing room and sat down next to Courtenay on the little carpeted bench.

"I've seen you before," he said as she sniffled. "I've noticed you hanging around my high school. I figured you must really want to meet me, you've been around so much!"

Courtenay smiled a little at the joke, and Brian had never seen anything so gorgeous in his life.

"You have a funny accent," she said. "Where are you from?"

"Switzerland," Brian said. "My family just moved here."

"Oh. Well, how do you like America?"

"So far, so good. But nobody told me there would be television stars hiding in all the dressing rooms!"

Courtenay smiled again. Then she laughed. Brian felt his heart thud in his chest.

"Here, let me," Brian said, taking the pink tissue away from her and dabbing at her eyes. He sang a few words from a lullaby his mom used to sing him, and Courtenay smiled again.

"Now, what were you thinking about, here in the dressing room?" he asked.

"Oh." Courtenay looked sad again. "I don't know. Nothing, really."

Brian remembered the horrible fight he had listened in on when he was outside Courtenay's trailer. Suddenly he felt kind of bad. Their fight was none of his business!

But another thought started growing slowly in his mind. What was it Joe had been complaining about? Courtenay didn't have time for him—she was too busy with her own life. Suddenly Brian realized that he could use the information from that fight to get Courtenay to go out with him! In her weakened, post-fight state, she wouldn't be able to say no. *Especially* if he poured on the killer Keller charm.

"Well, whatever it is, I'll bet your boyfriend can make you feel better," Brian said sympathetically.

Courtenay sighed. "Actually, he's the problem!" she admitted. "He's being a total jerk." She got up suddenly and wandered into the store, looking distractedly at the expensive dresses.

"Well, he's a fool," Brian declared, following her out of the dressing room and doing his best to sound shocked and surprised.

"You think so?" Courtenay stopped sorting through a pile of scarves and looked at Brian.

"Definitely," he said. "If I was your boyfriend, I wouldn't let us have such a stupid fight."

"You wouldn't?" They walked slowly around the store, then out the door into the main part of the mall.

"No way! I would be totally content to hang back if you had something you had to do. It would be worth it."

"Really?" Courtenay was looking intrigued. *That old Keller magic*, Brian thought, cheering himself on.

"Really," he said aloud. "In fact, if I left you alone for a whole afternoon . . . if I was selfish enough to go surfing or something . . . I would expect you to go out with someone else."

"You would?" Courtenay looked surprised for a second, then a little bit indignant.

"Uh-huh." Brian nodded.

Courtenay was quiet as the mall music played softly in the background. "Well, thanks," she finally said. "I mean, for listening and everything. It's been a long time since someone has been so honest with me."

"Don't mention it," Brian said, feeling a tiny pang of guilt.

"Well, I'd better get back to the set," she said. "I snuck away from my bodyguards, and they're going to be looking for me."

"Oh, okay. Well, it was nice meeting you," Brian

said. "My name is Brian Keller, by the way." He stuck out his hand for her to shake.

"I'm Courtenay Amour," she said, shaking his hand.

"Really?" he said, and they both laughed.

"Hey, listen. I know you're probably busy," he said, mentally moving in for the kill. "But the Palisades Carnival opens this week. Since we're both new to Palisades, why don't we go together? Say, Thursday night?"

Courtenay looked dubious, then her expression grew thoughtful. "He should expect me to go out with someone else," she said softly.

"I beg your pardon?" Brian asked.

"Nothing." Courtenay flashed him a brilliant smile. "I'd love to go to the carnival with you."

Brian was ready to drop dead with happiness. The beautiful, the perfect, the awesome Courtenay Amour was going to go out with him! Then it all got even better. She hopped up onto her tiptoes and planted a kiss right on his nose!

Brian closed his eyes. He thought he saw a brilliant flash of light as her lips touched the end of his nose. *Wow, she must be a great kisser*, he thought. *I think I'm seeing fireworks!*

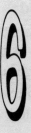

chapter

6

On Wednesday morning, Megan waited anxiously in front of her locker. She was supposed to meet Dave before class so that they could spend some quality time together. But the first bell was about to ring. Where was he?

Finally she saw him coming toward her. He held a sheet of plastic-covered paper in his hand.

"Hey, Megan!" he greeted her as he gave her a quick peck on the lips. "Here, I made this for you."

"What is it?" Megan asked, taking the paper.

"It's an illustrated outline of the human circulatory system," he explained. "I did a whole series of these for my science-fair project. What do you think?"

Megan looked at the beautifully colored, intricately

drawn diagram. It was hard to believe that the picture showed what her insides looked like. Dave had worked really hard on it, and it had won first prize at the science fair. Megan was touched that he was giving it to her. "It's very thoughtful," she said, slipping her hand into his. "How is your new project going?"

"Pretty well," he replied. "How's your studying for the SATs going?"

"Okay, I guess. I mean, it's going *favorably*."

Dave laughed. "Is that a vocabulary word?"

"Affirmative," Megan answered. Just then, the bell rang.

"First period," Dave said apologetically. "I'll see you later!" He gave her a kiss on the forehead and hurried down the hallway.

"See you later," Megan said as she watched him disappear around the corner. She slipped the drawing he'd given her into her locker. "Nice spending time with you," she added to the small picture of him hanging on the locker door. She closed the door with a sigh and headed to class.

"Miss Jones!" a familiar voice said behind her. She turned around to see Mr. Belding rushing toward her, his jacket flapping a little as he trotted down the hall. He held a chubby finger up in the air. "Un momento, por favor!" he announced with a fractured Spanish accent.

"Hi, Mr. Belding," she said, smiling at him. "What's up?"

The principal caught up to Megan and fell into step beside her. "Courtenay's parents tell me that things didn't go so well in the library yesterday," he said apologetically.

"Oh, it wasn't so bad," Megan replied, her heart skipping a beat. Was Mr. Belding going to let her off the hook? Maybe she wasn't going to have to tutor that prima donna anymore!

"That's nice of you to say, but from what I understand, Courtenay was very rude."

"Well, I guess she was pretty out of line," Megan admitted.

"And I'm sure you tried your best," Mr. Belding said. "I hope you don't feel too bad that it didn't work out."

"Anything for Bayside, Mr. Belding." Megan nodded. She was feeling a hundred times lighter. No more Courtenay!

"I knew that was how you would feel, and that's why I convinced Courtenay's parents to give you one more chance!" He clapped his hands and gave Megan a big smile, as if he had just told her that summer vacation was going to start a month early.

"*What?*" Megan stopped walking and stared at him.

"I knew you'd be pleased," Mr. Belding giggled, dancing a little jig. "They wanted to cancel the whole tutoring program and give up, but I wouldn't let them. I just knew you'd want to give it the old college try!"

"Speaking of the old college try, Mr. Belding, the SATs—"

"You're going to ace the SATs, no problem!" Mr. Belding said, clapping her on the back. "You guys can meet today after school in the library."

He toddled away from her before she could object again. "Megan Jones, Bayside's Hollywood connection!" he sang as he disappeared around the corner.

"Fabulous," Megan said sarcastically. "Just fabulous."

o o o

In first-period English class, Brian was struggling to stay awake as Mr. Hungadunga, his teacher, outlined the plot of *A Tale of Two Cities*.

"Meanwhile, Madame Defarge was knitting a sweater," the teacher droned in a flat monotone. "This is to be of great importance in the later parts of the plot."

"Psst."

Brian's eyes snapped open as he felt a wet spray at the back of his neck. He wiped at it and looked up at the ceiling. Was there something wrong with the sprinkler system?

"*Psst.*"

He heard it again. This time he checked under his chair. Maybe it was a noise from the auto shop outside the school.

"*Pssssst!*"

This time his chair moved violently as someone kicked it. Brian turned around to see Bobby, who had come in a few minutes late.

"What's the matter, is someone letting the air out of you?" he whispered.

"I was trying to get your attention, you dope," Bobby whispered back.

"Well, you have it now," Brian said, checking anxiously to be sure Mr. Hungadunga hadn't heard them talking. "What's up?"

"I want to show you the T-shirt I got Grizelda," Bobby whispered. He poked Brian in the side, and Brian reached down and took the shirt from him, spreading it out on his lap carefully.

The picture looked terrible! Brian had to hold his breath to keep from laughing out loud. Bobby had been in a big hurry, all right. It looked as if they had snapped the picture of him as he ran out of the store. He was kind of scrunched down in the corner of the picture, waving happily. He wasn't even in focus.

"It's great, Bobby," Brian whispered over his shoulder. He looked at the shirt again. Then he did a double take, and his blood ran cold.

There, in the background of the picture—next to Bobby's left ear—was Brian . . . getting a kiss from Courtenay!

Brian squinted and looked closely at the picture. It was definitely him, in his blue jeans and striped rugby shirt. Courtenay was on her tiptoes, brushing the tip of his nose with her lips. They were standing in front of the clothing store where he had met her in the dressing room.

He realized with a shock that they had taken the picture of Bobby at the exact moment of the kiss. That explained the flash of light! The light wasn't the result of Courtenay's stellar kissing skills. It was a photographic flash! And Brian's greatest moment was immortalized on 100 percent cotton!

Brian's face broke into a broad grin. He was about to turn around and show off his moment of triumph when he realized something else.

This shirt was for Grizelda. Grizelda tutored

Rachel. And if Rachel saw this shirt, with a picture of Brian enjoying a kiss from another girl, she'd never go out with him!

He knew what he had to do. He had to choose between the woman of his dreams and the hottest girl in Hollywood.

Or did he? If he could keep Rachel from seeing this shirt, she wouldn't know about his date with Courtenay. Oh, she'd probably find out about it eventually. But she'd already be his girlfriend by then. She'd be so entranced by the Keller charm, she wouldn't care about one date.

He had to keep her from seeing the shirt!

"I don't know, Bobby," Brian whispered back over his shoulder. "I wouldn't give this to her if I were you."

"Why not?" Bobby whispered back, sounding hurt.

"You're all out of focus," Brian told him. "She can't tell how handsome you are!"

Bobby grabbed the shirt and studied it carefully.

"You really think so?" he asked.

"Definitely," Brian affirmed.

Bobby thought about it for a minute. "I'm giving it to her anyway," he finally said. "It may be out of focus, but it has character. And she can see how handsome I am in person!" He grinned happily as Brian twisted around in his seat, looking at him pleadingly.

"Besides," Bobby went on. "If it really showed me looking my best, the real me might not be enough for her." He nodded happily. "But thanks for the input, my Swiss mister!" He patted Brian on the shoulder.

Brian turned around and slumped down in his chair. He tried to concentrate on Mr. Hungadunga, but he couldn't. All he could think of was that stupid shirt! He had to get his hands on it. But how?

○ ○ ○

"Megan Jones, please report to the principal's office. Megan Jones, to the office!"

"Well! That's twice in one week, Megan," Ms. Heller said brightly.

"Huh?" Megan asked, looking up from a half-dissected frog. It was lab day in biology class, Megan's favorite class of the week.

"You just got called to Mr. Belding's office. Didn't you hear?"

Megan put down her lab tools reluctantly. What could Mr. Belding possibly want from her now?

"Can't we just pretend we didn't hear that announcement?" she asked her teacher.

"I don't think so," Ms. Heller answered with a smile. "But don't worry, I'm sure it's something minor."

Easy for you to say, Megan thought sourly. *You get*

to go home at the end of the day. I have to stick around and play Insult the Tutor with the worst student on network television!

She was sure Mr. Belding was going to be waiting for her with some new request or responsibility. Maybe Courtenay wanted her to wear clown makeup. Or maybe she wanted to be tutored at three in the morning. How far was Mr. Belding going to push her?

But Mr. Belding wasn't in the office at all. Instead, Ms. Sansone, the secretary, was holding the telephone out to her.

"Emergency phone call for you," she said.

Emergency?

"Hello?" Megan said into the phone.

"Hi, honey," her mother's voice answered. "Don't worry! Nothing terrible has happened. I had to say it was an emergency to get you out of class."

"What is it, then?" Megan asked, her heart flooding with relief.

"I just got a call from Mr. Hansen, and I can't leave work right now," she said. "And your dad's in the middle of a trial."

"Mr. Hansen? I don't get it," Megan said. Why would their neighbor be calling her mom at work?

"Well, Trouble escaped again, and he dug up Mr. Hansen's flower bed. He's fit to be tied. When Trouble destroyed his rosebushes, he said he was going to call the police!"

"I remember," Megan said, beginning to panic again.

"Megan, I can't keep worrying about this!" Mrs. Jones sighed on the other end of the phone. "You've got to get that dog under control. Or else . . . we might have to give him away."

"No!" Megan cried. "Mom, you can't do that. I promise, in a week or two, I'll have more time to train him!"

"Sweetie, you're a busy girl. I know you've wanted a dog forever, but maybe Trouble is the wrong dog for you."

Megan thought of her big, galumphing mutt and his huge brown eyes. She imagined him being packed into a station wagon and taken to some farm, where they wouldn't know that kibbles were his favorite food. Where no one would know about that special spot on his tummy where he liked to be scratched! Her eyes filled with tears.

"Mom, no. I'll take care of it! I promise. I'll get Mr. Hansen off your back, and I'll take care of Trouble!"

Megan's mother sighed again. "Well, we'll talk about it tonight. Right now someone has to get Trouble out of Mr. Hansen's backyard."

"No problem," Megan assured her. "I'll go over there right away."

She handed the phone back to Ms. Sansone, who nodded to Megan that she was free to leave. Megan shot out the door, anxious to get to her neighbor's house.

It was up to her to save Trouble!

"Please, Mr. Hansen, don't call the police! I promise Trouble won't bother you anymore."

Mr. Hansen was a thin, fussy man who lived with his wife. Their lawn was always cut to exactly one and three-quarters inches, their curtains were starched and pressed, and the inside of their house was always clean and neat. They didn't have any kids or pets.

Mr. Hansen crossed his skinny arms across his chest and shook his head. He was surrounded by complete and total destruction.

All of the flowers had been dug up and tossed haphazardly around the yard—their rainbow-colored corpses dotted the lawn. There was a huge hole in the beautifully manicured grass, and it looked as if

Trouble had rolled around in it, kicking up huge piles of dirt. Two bushes had been pulled over. Trouble had even managed to knock down a bird feeder. A line of alarmed-looking birds peeked down from the branches of a tree—the only thing left standing in the poor, hassled backyard. Megan couldn't quite believe that her overgrown puppy had caused all this damage, but his nose and paws verified his guilt. They were covered with dirt!

"I'm so sorry about your flowers," Megan said. "I'll pay for new ones!" She held on for dear life to Trouble's collar. He was trying to jump up and kiss her. He also seemed to want to show her the great job he'd done rearranging this boring backyard. He bounded around in a circle while Megan clung to him, trying to keep a conversation going with her cranky neighbor.

"Pay for new ones! That's ridiculous," Mr. Hansen snapped in a raspy voice. "The bulbs are quite expensive. I order them from Holland."

"Well, I'll write to Holland and tell them what happened," Megan continued desperately. "Maybe they'll send you some new ones. Maybe my dad could help! He's a judge, you know. . . ."

"I am well aware of your father's legal connections," Mr. Hansen intoned. His eyes bored straight through

Megan, making her feel like a flimsy paper doll. "His position will not stop me from taking action. That dog is a menace!" He pointed a shaky finger at Trouble.

Right on cue, sensing that someone was angry at him, Trouble whimpered and lay down. He put his head on his two front paws and wagged his tail. He looked first at Mr. Hansen, then at Megan, then back again. He just didn't understand what he had done wrong! Megan wanted to get down on her knees and give him a big kiss, he looked so sorry.

But Mr. Hansen was unmoved. "It is now three-thirty," he said. "I am calling the authorities. Depending on their response time, and the time it takes me to make out my report, I should be arriving at your house at—"

"Three-thirty!" Megan yelped. Trouble sat up.

"That is the time now," Mr. Hansen repeated. "It will take me—"

"Mr. Hansen, I just remembered, I'm supposed to be doing something really important right now!"

He turned his watery eyes to her again. "I fail to see what is more important than—"

"I know. I'm really sorry! I promise I'll keep Trouble out of your hair from now on, okay? Okay! Great!" Megan babbled, dragging her dog out of the backyard.

Trouble seemed to have lost interest in his project, so she was able to get him home pretty quickly. She shoved him through the kitchen door and ran to the phone. She dialed the number for the Bayside office.

"Trouble!" she called sharply. He looked up briefly from the old sneaker he was chewing, then returned to his work. The phone rang a few times on the other end of the line.

"This is Mr. Belding," she finally heard her principal answer.

"Oh, Mr. Belding, thank goodness. This is Megan Jones!" she said in a rush. She heard a few loud noises from the next room, but the cord didn't reach far enough for her to go check it out.

"I'm supposed to be tutoring Courtenay this afternoon, but I had to come home," she went on.

"I know, I know. Nothing wrong, I hope? You're not ill?"

"Oh no, I'm fine," she said. "It's just, my dog kind of ran amok and I had to get him out of my neighbor's flower bed."

"Well! All taken care of?" Mr. Belding said brightly.

"Yeah, pretty much," Megan said.

"Well, I can see you're not going to want to come all the way back to Bayside this afternoon."

"No, that wouldn't really be convenient," Megan agreed.

"So we'll just send Courtenay over to you!" he finished.

"*What*?" Megan cried. She heard a loud crash from the next room, then the sound of four running feet tearing through the front hall and into the dining room.

"*I said, we'll send her over to you*," Mr. Belding shouted into the phone. "I think we have a bad connection," he said to someone else in the office. "She sounds as if she's in a war zone!"

"Mr. Belding, wait!" Megan squeaked. But the line went dead as he hung up the phone. She sank into a chair and put her head down on the kitchen table with a groan.

There was another crash, and a yelp from the dining room. Megan shot out of her chair and ran into the front hall, looking for Trouble.

She found trouble, all right.

Her house looked like Mr. Hansen's backyard. In those few minutes, her dog had managed to destroy her mother's favorite lamp, knock over the umbrella stand, spill the contents of three houseplants (including her dad's prize ficus), and flip one of the upholstered dining-room chairs over on himself. He blinked up at her, helplessly pinned.

"Are you okay?" she asked, picking up the chair.

"*Rowf*," he answered.

o o o

Brian sat at the open window, concentrating. The classroom was totally empty—the last bell had rung five minutes before. Most of the Bayside students—including Bobby and Grizelda—were chilling in the schoolyard, outside this window. Brian took a deep breath and stuck his fishing rod through the window.

Slowly, painstakingly, Brian began to lower his hook. Bobby carried his backpack on his back, and it was open. A brightly wrapped package was sticking out of it.

I'm a genius, Brian thought. *I'm like James Bond!* He lowered the hook even more. It got closer . . . and closer. . . .

"Hey, Brian! Are you fishing for freshmen?" a perky voice called out behind him. Brian whirled around to see Lindsay and Tommy entering the classroom, holding hands. And Rachel was right behind them!

"Hey, what are you guys doing here?" he asked, trying to sound casual. He put down the fishing rod and leaned it against the wall. Peeking out the window, he saw Bobby pulling the present out of his backpack and handing it to Grizelda. He gulped and turned back to his friends, smiling a little queasily.

"Just looking for you," Lindsay said. "Well, Rachel was." Rachel smiled and blushed a little.

"What did we interrupt, here?" Tommy D. picked up the fishing rod.

"Oh, nothing," Brian replied, grabbing it from him. "Just a little physics experiment. I don't think it worked, though."

"Wow, physics! I didn't know you were a science whiz," Rachel said. She looked impressed.

"Well . . . yeah, I guess I am," Brian stammered. *Sure, a science whiz. Whatever works*, he thought.

"I guess we'll let you off the hook," Lindsay said. She and Tommy giggled together at the joke, and Rachel moved closer to Brian.

"I found the little teddy bear in my makeup case," she whispered in his ear. "Thank you."

"No problem," he said gallantly. "I knew I put it in a place where you'd find it!"

She smiled dazzlingly. "I accept," she said.

"Great!" Brian said. Hearing those words from a beautiful girl was always a good thing. He was mystified, though. What was she accepting?

70

"I'd love to go to the carnival with you tomorrow night," she added.

Then he remembered with a flash. He had put the note in her makeup bag the day before—before he made a date with Courtenay *for Thursday night at the carnival!*

How could he have let this happen? Two beautiful dates was great . . . but on the same night? He was in deep trouble!

Rachel smiled and leaned over, kissing him lightly on the cheek. "It was very sweet."

"Like you," he said absently.

Rachel giggled. "We're going to the Max; you want to come?" she asked brightly. Brian was about to accept when he saw his fishing line jerk a few times. It looked like he had caught something. Was it the shirt, after all? Maybe it had gotten snagged from Grizelda's backpack. . . .

"I can't go right now," he said. "I'll come by after my experiment is done, okay?" he added when Rachel gave him a little pout. The line tugged a little harder. Brian wished they would leave so that he could see what he had caught!

"Okay, we'll see you after your experiment," Rachel agreed. She flashed him another brilliant smile, then vanished out the door with Lindsay and Tommy. Brian immediately spun around, and started reeling in his catch.

"Come on, T-shirt," he prayed out loud. "Come to Brian, you ugly, incriminating rag. . . ."

Finally, the hook was close enough to grab. He reached out the window and pulled it in. It wasn't the T-shirt, though. It was a small blue plastic box with something rattling around in it.

BOBBY'S RETAINER, a little label announced.

"Blech!" Brian yipped, dropping his gross prize. He stuck his head out the window, hoping that Bobby would still be there. Maybe he could try again!

But Bobby was nowhere in sight. And the empty wrapping paper lay in a crumpled heap at the bottom of a garbage can.

"So much for James Bond," Brian sighed. Grizelda had the T-shirt, so Rachel was bound to see it. And he had two dates for the carnival! Now what was he going to do?

o o o

Megan was scooping the last bit of dirt into one of the half-dead houseplants when the doorbell rang. She looked at her wristwatch—was it already time for Courtenay to be here?

The doorbell rang again, and Megan took a quick

look around. She had tried to clean up, but the place still looked pretty awful. And Trouble was crying and scratching at the bathroom door.

"I'm coming," she yelled, running to the front door.

Courtenay breezed right past Megan as if she were walking into her own house. She dropped her leather book bag carelessly by the door.

"Come on in," Megan muttered as Courtenay looked around the living room.

Megan's family lived comfortably, and they had a nice house. It was professionally decorated, and a cleaning woman came every week to keep it in tip-top shape. Still, it bothered Megan that Courtenay was giving it a once-over. Who did she think she was?

"Maybe we should start studying," Megan suggested.

"*Rowf*," Trouble yelped from the bathroom.

"What was that?" Courtenay asked, looking around.

Oh, great, Megan thought. *It's bad enough she thinks my house is a dump. Now Trouble is going to make all kinds of noise.*

"*Awoo*," Trouble whined.

"It's a dog," Courtenay said.

Right on cue, Trouble scratched at the door. Before Megan could stop her, Courtenay opened the bath-room door and let Trouble loose.

He leaped out of the bathroom like a cannon, knocking Courtenay on her butt. Then he put his front paws on her shoulders and started licking her face happily.

"Oh my gosh, are you okay?" Megan asked, trying to pull Trouble off. She tugged desperately at his collar. *Now she's really going to freak out—a strange mutt slobbering all over her!*

"Oooh!" Courtenay sang out. At first, Megan thought she was trying to wriggle out from under Trouble. But after half a second, it was clear what Courtenay was doing.

She was cuddling Trouble!

Trouble turned over onto his back. Courtenay found his special scratching spot almost immediately, and he rolled his eyes happily as she attacked it with her perfectly manicured nails. He reached up and gave her a wet, slobbery kiss, and she buried her TV-star face in his filthy fur.

"*Oooo*such a *big* doggie, who's a *dirty* doggie?" she crowed, and he wagged his tail as if she were reciting his favorite dog poetry.

"Excuse me?" Megan asked. She was still trying to figure out what was going on.

"I'm sorry," Courtenay said, looking up. Trouble stuck his giant head into her lap and stretched out as she continued to scratch him. "I never get to hang out with dogs anymore. Is it okay if I pet him?"

"Sure." Megan shrugged. She sat down next to Trouble, a few feet away from Courtenay. The actress had a big, dirty smudge across her face, where Trouble had rubbed against her. She didn't seem to care.

"What do you mean, 'anymore'?" Megan asked.

"My parents owned a dog-obedience school when I was a kid," she said. "I loved having all those dogs around all the time! But when my career really took off, they sold the school and became my managers full-time. It's like, they forgot that they ever did anything that didn't revolve around me. They totally forgot how much fun we used to have." She scratched a spot behind Trouble's ear, and he wiggled and shook his leg.

"Sounds like you really miss it," Megan said.

"I'd love to have a big cutie like this to hang out with," Courtenay said with a smile. "You're really lucky."

"I don't feel lucky! He's totally uncontrollable. I won't be able to keep him if he keeps destroying stuff the way he does."

"Oh no!" Courtenay's eyes opened wide with horror. "You have to train him!"

Megan snorted. "You think I haven't tried? He's a big dummy. It's hopeless!"

"It's never hopeless," Courtenay said, shaking her head earnestly. Megan couldn't believe this was the same girl who had been staring blankly off into space the day before!

Courtenay sprang up and stood firmly on two feet, her hands on her hips. Trouble jumped up, too, and started running around, hoping she was going to play.

"*Sssssssssssit-ah!*" she spat commandingly. She held her hand up in the air, pointing down. Trouble cocked his head at her quizzically.

"*Sssit!*" she said again, pushing his hind end down gently and repeating the sound and motion. He sat and looked back at her. *Is this right?* he seemed to be saying.

"*Sit,*" she announced, smiling at him. He sat calmly and thumped his tail on the floor again. Courtenay lowered her hand into a "stop" position.

"Stay," she said. Trouble held his head high and stayed right where he was.

"That is amazing," Megan said, getting up and standing next to Courtenay. "I can't even get him to stand still when he's eating!"

"He wants to make you happy," Courtenay

explained. "You just have to be really clear about what you want him to do."

"I never thought about it like that," Megan said, nodding. Trouble was looking at her. "You want to make me happy, doggie?" He answered her with a few happy thumps of his tail. She knelt down next to the dog and scratched the special spot between his ears.

"You know, you're really good at this," she told Courtenay.

"Thanks," Courtenay said. She smiled again, and Megan thought she actually looked like a nice person—now that she was just being herself.

"Hey, do you think you could help me out with him? After we do our tutoring?"

"You mean, a little dog tutoring?" Courtenay asked. Then she laughed at her own joke. "Sure!"

Megan grinned. Courtenay, making a joke! She was starting to think that there might actually be a cool person behind those blue eyes!

On Thursday morning, Megan was at her locker, picking out the books she was going to need for her first few classes. *LoveSchool* had moved to a different part of Bayside, so this hallway was pretty much back to normal. Everyone was milling around, talking and yelling. It was a regular, high school kind of noise, the kind of noise you don't even notice—until it stops.

When the hall went silent, Megan looked up. It was eerie—people just stopped talking and started staring! It took her a few seconds to figure out what was going on. Then she saw Courtenay walking down the hallway toward her. All eyes were on the blond beauty as she came over to Megan, her face frozen in a fake little smile, her eyes carefully trained on the ground. It looked like she was trying to act as if everything were totally normal. Except that she was in the middle of about a hundred watchful eyes.

Wow, that's really creepy, Megan thought. *It's like she's a thing, not a person. . . . No wonder she acted so weird when I first met her.*

"Hi, Courtenay," Megan called out, breaking the silence. Courtenay looked up, smiled a *real* smile, and gratefully waved back.

"Hey, Megan," she said, arriving at the locker. "Mr. Belding told me your locker was on this floor, so I figured I'd come up and see you between scenes!"

Slowly, people stopped staring and started going about their regular business. They were still sort of looking sideways at Courtenay, but were also talking to one another, getting their books, and doing whatever they had been doing before she walked into the hall.

"Well, that's cool," Megan said, trying to make Courtenay feel as normal as possible. "Thanks again for all your help last night."

"Can you believe how great that was?" Courtenay gushed. "Trouble is really a smart dog. I think he loved confusing those people!"

Courtenay was still totally excited about their successful training session with Trouble. By the time Mr. Hansen had arrived with two animal-control officers,

Trouble was willing to sit still. In fact, he was angelic! The animal-control people had apologized for taking up Megan's time, and told Mr. Hansen that the dog definitely didn't look like a menace. All they did was give Megan a warning. And Megan was sure that with a little more training, Trouble would be well behaved. He wouldn't be bothering anyone else's shrubbery.

"Yeah, it was really great. . . ." Megan started to feel a bit uncomfortable. Courtenay was just standing there, looking expectantly at her. "Is there something else? I mean, is anything bothering you? Or did you just come to say hi?"

Courtenay let out a long sigh. "I'm not really good at this," she admitted. "I'm not used to hanging out with people that aren't part of Hollywood, you know? But I kind of need to talk to someone."

"Well, you can talk to me!" Megan assured her. "After all, you saved my dog. What's up?"

Courtenay looked grateful. "It's just—" She thought for a minute. "You know I'm dating Joe, right?"

"Right." Megan nodded.

"Well, we had this horrible fight the other day. We're both really busy, and we're on, like, opposite schedules, so we never get to see each other. And we were supposed to spend the afternoon together, the day of my second tutoring session with you."

80

"Oh, no wonder you were so bummed about being there," Megan said.

"Yeah, that's why I was so distracted," Courtenay said, laughing. "You should have smacked me in the head!"

"What, and get sued by your director? No thanks!" Megan laughed back.

"So I got totally mad at him, because he was being too demanding. I tried to explain that I wanted to hang out with him, but I didn't have time. He just got mad! So after the fight, another guy asked me out, and I said yes."

"Well, it's okay to go on a date. Especially if you guys are fighting," Megan said.

"But I don't even want to! I want to get things back on track with Joe, only he won't even talk to me!"

"Yowza, what a bummer," Megan said, shaking her head.

"Gee, thanks for the great advice," Courtenay said, smiling ruefully.

"No, I mean—" Megan started to apologize, then realized Courtenay was just kidding. She laughed again. It was weird, finding out that this two-dimensional image from television had a real personality!

"What I mean is," Megan went on, "I've been having the same kind of problem with my boyfriend. We're not fighting or anything, but we don't have any time together!"

"So what are you doing about it?" Courtenay wanted to know.

"Nothing, so far," Megan admitted, and Courtenay's face fell. "It's not the kind of problem you can solve between classes at someone's locker," Megan added, getting an idea. "But it is the kind of problem that a good dose of girl talk can cure!"

"Girl talk? I thought that only happened on TV!" Courtenay said with a grin.

Megan shook her head. "Oh, it happens in real life," she said. "You just have to have the right friends."

o o o

"Make way for Bobby's girlfriend! Hey! Hey, everybody! Move out of the way, it's *my girlfriend*!"

It was later that day. Bobby was walking down the hallways of Bayside, arms out at his side, making sure nobody jostled Grizelda. She proudly wore her birthday T-shirt, with Bobby smiling and waving smack in the middle of her belly.

Suddenly Bobby spotted Brian, and his eyes lit up.

"Ah-ha!" he yelped. He grabbed Grizelda's hand, kissed it, and raced over to Brian.

"Well?" Bobby demanded. Grizelda looked kind of stunned, but happy.

Brian had no idea what was expected of him. "Well what?" he asked.

"Well what?" Bobby repeated. "Well—what do you have to say for yourself? You told me not to give Grizelda the T-shirt. But I did! And now she's my girlfriend!" He crossed his arms over his chest and smiled triumphantly. "Tell him, sweet thing," he said to Grizelda.

"It's true," she said. "I already thought he was kind of sweet, even though his little surprises didn't always work quite right. And the shirt was just so cute, I had to say yes!" She wrinkled her nose and smiled at Bobby, who looked like he was about to bust.

"I guess I was wrong," Brian said, feeling his heart sink as he looked at the shirt. It was so obvious. He couldn't take his eyes off the image of him getting a kiss from Courtenay. Rachel was bound to see it!

"Well, congratulations, you two lovebirds," he said, trying to smile. But Bobby and Grizelda were gazing into each other's eyes, ignoring him completely.

"Okay, well . . . see you later," he added, moving around them.

"See ya," they answered in unison, still mooning at each other.

"Whoops!" Grizelda suddenly snapped to attention. "I have to get to Rachel's locker. I'm meeting her for lunch, so we can go over some of her computer lessons!"

"You can't leave me," Bobby cried, dropping to his knees and clinging to her waist.

"It's just for lunch, Bobby," she answered, playfully swatting him away. "I'll meet you right after, okay?"

Sheesh. Brian couldn't believe how the world worked sometimes! Here he was, the king of the Casanovas, trapped in a romantic nightmare. Meanwhile, Bobby the doofus made a couple of goofy, amateurish attempts at romance, and all of a sudden he was living on Planet Love with the woman of his dreams! It didn't seem right!

Brian wasn't sure how he was going to deal with the fact that he had two dates that night . . . but he would do his best to keep them from finding out about each other. And as long as Grizelda was wearing that shirt, he had to keep Rachel away from Grizelda.

Brian looked at the index card in his wallet, where he had written down Rachel's schedule. He'd have to race to her classroom to keep her away from this tutoring session!

Third floor. Wouldn't you know it! Brian cursed his luck as he bounded up the stairs, hoping to catch

84

Rachel still in class. With any luck, he'd be able to sweep her away from her appointment with Grizelda! He raced out of the stairwell and down the hallway.

"Brian! Are you okay?"

Brian looked up—Rachel was right in front of him!

"You look like you've been running a marathon," she said, her blue eyes full of concern.

"Wanted to catch you," he huffed. "Lunch with me?"

"I'm supposed to meet Grizelda," she objected.

Over her shoulder, all the way down the hall, Brian could see Grizelda just rounding the corner. Brian didn't think she'd seen Rachel yet.

"Come here," he said, grabbing Rachel by the hand and yanking her into another hallway. He dragged her up another flight of stairs, finally ending up in a deserted corner of the school.

"Hey!" Rachel giggled. "Be careful—you're going to pull my arm out of its socket!"

"Sorry," he said, hoping Grizelda hadn't seen them. "I had something to show you."

"Well? What is it?" Rachel asked.

"What is what?" Now Brian was really confused.

"What did you have to show me?"

"Oh!" Brian looked around. There wasn't much there, except a garbage can, some graffiti, and a doorway. He didn't know where it went. But it was all he had.

"I wanted to show you this," he said, pushing open the door and hoping it was something good.

"Oooh!" Rachel exclaimed, her eyes widening. Brian turned around and saw that he had found an old, forgotten entrance to the roof of Bayside. All of Palisades lay stretched out in front of them, in brilliant springtime colors.

"What a romantic spot," Rachel said, stepping past him to stand on the tar-paper roof. She leaned on the railing and looked out. Then she turned back to him, smiling sweetly.

"This is really a wonderful lunchtime surprise," she said, flashing him a smile.

"Yeah, it was a surprise to me, too," he said, propping the door open with the garbage can and stepping out to stand next to her. "I mean, when I found it, I was surprised."

"Oh, Brian," Rachel sighed, leaning her head on his shoulder. "I think I'm really falling for you!"

Brian knew he should be totally savoring this moment, but it was kind of hard to enjoy when he knew there was more trouble coming. Sure, he was safe for now . . . but there was still the matter of that night's date.

Maybe his charm was working *too* well!

chapter

9

"**M**egan, when are you going to tell me what's going on?" Lindsay demanded.

"Yeah, what's the big secret?" Rachel wanted to know.

"Just hold on a second," Megan replied, checking behind her to make sure no one was around. The hallway was deserted, and so was the *Beacon* office. This part of the school was currently *LoveSchool* territory, but this hallway wasn't being used.

"Okay. I have a friend, and she needs some help. But you have to promise not to freak out, and you can't tell anyone!" Megan stated.

"Megan! Who are we going to tell? Come on, you're acting really weird!" Lindsay looked totally exasperated.

"Okay, okay. Come on in." Megan swung the door to an empty classroom open and Lindsay walked in. Then she stopped short.

"*Whoa.*" Lindsay just stood there, staring. She looked like a statue.

Megan scooted around her and passed her hand over Lindsay's eyes. "Hello? Lindsay? Anybody home?" Megan asked.

"It's Courtenay Amour," Lindsay whispered loudly.

"Yes, it is," Megan whispered back. "And she's a real person, not a TV image, so she can hear everything you say!"

Lindsay shook her head a little, trying to clear it. It was too bizarre! She was used to seeing this girl on television every week. Lately, she had seen her around school, but always at a distance. Now she was sitting right in front of her!

Meanwhile, Rachel was just standing there with both her hands over her mouth. She was making a weird squeaking noise.

"Rachel?" Megan knocked on her head.

"Revlon!" she blurted out, pointing at Courtenay.

"What?" Now Courtenay looked confused.

"Revlon Oil-Free Base. Right?" Rachel moved in closer and peered at Courtenay's eyelashes. "And Maybelline. No! Wait. Cover Girl mascara!"

88

Courtenay laughed. "Really, I don't know. They put the makeup on me. If I had my way, I wouldn't wear any makeup at all."

"Don't even say that!" Rachel objected. She gazed at Courtenay for a few more seconds, then sat down at one of the desks. "Wow, you are prettier than me," she said wonderingly. Then she put her hand over her mouth, totally embarrassed. What a doofy thing to say!

Courtenay just laughed. "Well, thanks," she said. "I guess that's why they pay me the big bucks." She and Megan and Rachel laughed, but Lindsay just looked confused. And a little dazed. Megan patted her friend on the hand and led her to a desk.

"So much for not freaking out," Megan remarked with a grimace. "Lindsay, I was hoping you could help Courtenay with a problem she's having. It's the same kind of problem I'm having with Dave, so I thought we could all kind of talk about it."

"What's the matter?" Lindsay asked, suddenly looking concerned.

"It's Joe," Courtenay said. "We never have any time together, and it's causing a lot of friction between us. And I think I've been making it worse lately, with my snotty attitude. I feel awful!"

"Well, are you trying to break up with him?"

Lindsay asked. She was starting to act like herself again, forgetting that Courtenay was a famous person.

"No! I want to work things out," Courtenay exclaimed.

"Hmm." Lindsay started turning the problem over in her mind. "I've been thinking about this lately," she said. "The thing is, you want to do the things that are important to you. But sometimes, you have to compromise, too. The key is knowing when to compromise and when to stick up for yourself."

"But what if you stick up for yourself, and the guy just gets fed up and leaves?" Courtenay asked. "That's what I'm afraid is happening now!"

Lindsay shrugged. "I don't want to sound cold-blooded, but sometimes that happens. And if the guy can't handle compromising, he wasn't worth having in the first place!"

Courtenay groaned. "You sound just like my grandma," she muttered.

"And my mom," Megan added. "But it makes sense. We can't be ruled by what guys want from us."

"Right, because then we just become little girl-friend-robots," Lindsay said encouragingly. "And that's not really what they want."

"It's not?" Rachel asked.

"Not if they're decent guys," Megan said, nodding.

"That makes sense," Courtenay agreed. "But I would feel a lot better if I knew how Joe really felt. He's pretty mad at me, and I can't tell if he still loves me or if he just wants to break up."

"If only we could ask him," Megan said thoughtfully.

"Well . . ." Rachel looked like she was cooking up some kind of scheme.

"Uh-oh. I hear wheels turning," Megan said, shaking her head.

"I was just thinking—" Rachel began.

"All right!" Megan cheered.

"Well, we needed a little girl talk, right?" Rachel reasoned.

"Right." Courtenay grinned.

"So what Joe needs is a little guy talk. All we have to do is get Tommy to talk to him!"

"Oh, right," Lindsay said. "And what do we tell them, that we think they need to have a heart-to-heart?"

"Yeah, maybe we can get them to have a slumber party," Megan giggled. "We can put curlers in their hair and they can do each other's makeup!"

"You guys!" Rachel was exasperated. "You're not thinking like a boy. They'll talk about their feelings while they're talking about guy stuff. We just have to get them together and tell Tommy to talk to Joe about cars or something. Before you know it, they'll be talking about real things!"

"Hey, that just might work," Lindsay admitted.

"Rachel!" Courtenay was impressed. "Where did you learn that?"

Rachel shrugged. "It just came to me when I was doing my face aerobics one day."

"Face aerobics?" Lindsay echoed.

"Yeah, you know." Rachel opened her eyes, then squinted. She looked like a fish. "You build up the muscles in your face. Then you don't get wrinkles!"

The other girls dissolved into a fit of giggles.

"Go ahead, laugh at me!" Rachel huffed. "But when you guys are getting face-lifts and slathering Oil of Olay on your faces, my skin will be smooth and young looking!"

"Yeah, with your humongously overdeveloped eye muscles," Megan cracked. The thought of Rachel with huge biceps-eyes made everyone start giggling harder.

"Can you move my couch with your nose?" Lindsay giggled.

Finally, Rachel started laughing, too. The whole group was out-of-control laughing.

"Ow! My side hurts," Lindsay said, gasping for air as the girls finished up their giggle session.

"Well, at least we have a plan," Megan said.

"You guys will really do all that for me?" Courtenay wanted to know.

"What, getting Tommy to talk to Joe? Of course!" Lindsay said.

"But why?" Courtenay stared at them, wide-eyed.

"Why?" Lindsay was amazed. "I don't know—you're Megan's friend and you need a hand. I think it sounds like fun!"

"Wow." Courtenay shook her head. "Thanks, you guys."

"You're welcome." Megan felt weird. Why was Courtenay thanking them?

"I mean, this is like a new thing for me," Courtenay explained. "Most people who are nice to me are doing it because I'm famous. You guys make me feel like a real person!"

"You are a real person, you goof," Megan said.

"You just happen to be a real person with no need for face aerobics," Rachel added mournfully.

○ ○ ○

"Okay. Are you sure you've got it?" Tommy asked Courtenay. "You remember everything I told you?"

"Tommy, I remember," she insisted. "I'm going to fix it so you can talk to Joe. I remember the plan!"

She slipped a screwdriver up her sleeve and sauntered across the football field, heading for Joe's trailer. It was right next to hers, painted dark blue. None of the techies noticed her—she was just another member of the *LoveSchool* movie cast. Looking over her shoulder, she whisked up to the door of Joe's trailer. She fiddled briefly with the lock, then walked casually away.

A few minutes later, Joe headed for his trailer. "Okay, Tiny," Joe called over his shoulder to the security guard, "we'll play hoops a little later." Reaching his trailer door, Joe grabbed the handle and tried to open it. It stuck. He jiggled it a few times, then kicked it.

"Hey!" Joe exclaimed, running his hand through his curly hair. "My door's stuck."

That was Tommy's cue. "Really?" he said, stepping out from behind a nearby costume rack. "Let me take a look."

"Thanks, man," Joe said, kicking the door of his trailer a second time. "These trailers are cool to hang out in, but they're basically big metal hunks of junk."

"I see what you mean," Tommy agreed, his attention focused on the little screw that Courtenay had jammed into the door. "This thing isn't exactly built like a Mack truck."

"No kidding," Joe agreed. "Not like my Beauty."

Tommy was so busy fiddling with the door that he

didn't hear Joe's response. Courtenay had done her job a little *too* well. Finally, the door opened.

"Hey, thanks a lot, man," Joe said warmly. "Want to come in for a sec?" He stepped into the trailer and held the door open.

"Sure," Tommy replied. He looked over at Courtenay, winked, and walked inside.

"As soon as we're done filming, I'm going to head up the coast with Courtenay and Beauty," Joe said, grinning.

"Wait—you have two girlfriends?" Tommy shook his head. "Lindsay didn't read *that* in her *LoveSchool* fan magazine," he chuckled.

"Who's Lindsay?" Joe asked.

"Oh, she's my girlfriend." Tommy grinned. "She loves your show. I've never actually watched it, myself."

"Me neither." Joe grinned back. Then he pointed to a framed picture on the wall. It was a 1967 Mustang convertible, painted black. The picture was cut out from a magazine.

"Oh, man, I have that same picture in my locker! From the September issue of *Car and Driver*, right? I love that car!" Tommy exclaimed.

"Dude, that's my car," Joe said, running his finger up the frame lovingly.

"Not if I find it first," Tommy said.

"No, I mean, they took that picture in my driveway. That car belongs to me!"

"No way," Tommy said, impressed. He looked at the wall, where pictures of several other classic cars hung in frames.

"These, too?" he asked, almost afraid to hear the answer. No one could own all those cars without dying of happiness!

"Oh yeah." Joe nodded. "Those are all mine. But Beauty is my favorite."

"Man," Tommy said, shaking his head. "Now I understand why all those girls like you so much."

Joe gave a rueful chuckle. "I guess. It doesn't matter, though. All those girls don't mean anything when my girlfriend won't even talk to me."

"She won't?" Tommy pretended to be shocked. "What's up with that?"

"I don't know. Seems like lately she's got no time for me."

"Oh, man," Tommy laughed, shaking his head. "Do I know what that's like!"

o o o

"Brian, I can't," Rachel protested, blushing.

"Of course you can! If you want, I'll get training wheels put on," Brian offered, clutching the bicycle-built-for-two that he had rented. It was just after school, and people were walking by, curiously eyeing him and the bike.

"No, I mean, I know how to ride a bike," Rachel giggled. "But we've been together all day! I blew off my tutoring session at lunch, and the test is tomorrow. If I miss my after-school session, I'm dead meat!"

"I'll tutor you!" Brian insisted in a last-ditch effort. Grizelda was still wearing that shirt!

"You? Tutor me?" Rachel smiled and put a finger on Brian's nose. "Brian, you know as much about computers as Vice Principal Screech knows about fashion!"

"Hey, Screech is a sharp dresser!" Brian said weakly.

Just then Screech came barreling through the crowd of students.

"Mr. Belding!" he called. "Perhaps this scarlet cummerbund would add an elegant flair to your blue pinstripe suit." He made his way toward the *LoveSchool* movie set, where Mr. Belding was being used in another scene.

"Maybe not," Brian admitted.

"Don't look so glum!" Rachel tugged at his shirt. "I'll see you later on, at the carnival," she said brightly.

That's what's making me so glum! Brian thought as he watched Rachel head back into Bayside. *But I can't worry about that now. If I can't keep Rachel away from Grizelda, I'll have to figure out a way to keep Grizelda away from Rachel!*

"Hey, buddy," Bobby interrupted Brian's thoughts. "Can I show you the T-shirt again?" He proudly displayed Grizelda for the billionth time that day.

"I've seen the shirt," Brian groaned.

"What's the matter, Brian?" Grizelda asked sympathetically. "Aren't things going well with Rachel?"

"Oh, it's not that," Brian said, suddenly struck with a brilliant idea. "I'm just so worried."

"What are you worried about?" Bobby asked.

"The Ping-Pong tournament!" Brian said, shaking his head sadly. "I heard that Valley just got a new player. He's supposed to be a ringer—a real secret weapon!"

"What?" Bobby was horrified. He turned to Grizelda. "Do you know what that means?"

"It means they could beat us. They're the only team between Bayside and the championship!" She was equally upset.

"We have to call an emergency practice session," Bobby insisted. "And you've got to be there—you're the newest member of the team!"

"But what about Rachel?" Grizelda squeaked. "I'm supposed to tutor her!"

98

"Oh, she told me to tell you," Brian said slyly. "She can't make it. Something about a facial."

"Then I can go to the practice!" Grizelda grabbed Bobby's hand excitedly.

"Thanks for the hot tip, Keller!" Bobby said gratefully. A second later, the two Ping-Pong players took off for their practice room.

That was a close one, Brian thought, wiping his brow. All this scheming and planning could really wear a guy out! But at least he had successfully kept Rachel from seeing the incriminating T-shirt. Now all he had to do was keep Rachel and Courtenay from finding out about each other!

chapter

10

"**B**ut Brian, aren't you going to come on the Ferris wheel with me?" Rachel looked totally confused.

"I really want you to see how beautiful Palisades looks at night from all the way up there," he said, patting her hand. "But I'm afraid of heights!"

"But—" Rachel started to protest, and Brian closed the bar that held her in her seat. He handed a ticket to the attendant.

"I'll be waiting right here for you," he assured her. "Have a great time!" He waved as the giant wheel started turning, taking her up into the starry night sky.

Then he slipped five dollars into the attendant's hand. "Keep her up there for ten minutes," he whispered desperately as he took off for the Whirl-o-Matic ride, which was just coming to a halt. Courtenay wobbled out of her seat, trying to smooth her long hair.

"Is your stomach feeling better?" she asked.

"What?" Brian asked.

"You said you couldn't go on the Whirl-o-Matic because your stomach hurt," she said, looking a little annoyed.

"Oh, right." Brian laughed. "Too much cotton candy. Did you ever notice, it looks so light, but it just sits in your stomach?"

"I guess." Courtenay didn't look very happy at all. He took her hand, then scanned the sky anxiously, checking to make sure Rachel's Ferris-wheel car was still parked safely at the top.

"Brian? What are you looking at?" Courtenay asked. She couldn't help but notice that he was acting a little weird.

"Oh, I was looking for the Big Dipper," he said. "Aren't the stars beautiful?"

"Oh yes," Courtenay agreed, relaxing a little. She looked up at the sky, but a second later Brian was pulling her toward another ride.

"Well, that was nice," he said as they wove through the crowd. "Do you want to go through the Tunnel of Love?"

"I don't know," Courtenay began. "You know, I wanted to tell you some—"

"Great! Here you go," he said, dragging her over to the dark, romantic ride and steering her into a heart-shaped boat. "I'll meet you at the other side."

"What the— You want me to go through the Tunnel of Love without you?"

"I have to call my mom," Brian explained, handing over another ticket. *One date is expensive*, he thought. *But two could make me go broke!* He didn't wait around to see the angry look on Courtenay's face as the car wound into the dark tunnel.

"Wasn't the view from the Ferris wheel gorgeous?" he asked as Rachel climbed out of her car a few seconds later.

"Stunning," she agreed. "It would have been better if you came with me, though," she added.

"Well, how about the haunted house next?" Brian offered, taking her hand.

"Great! I love to be scared." Rachel snuggled close to Brian. "Will you be there to protect me?"

"Sure! I'll be right there when you get out of the haunted house," he offered.

Rachel blew her breath out sharply. She was really getting tired of this! It was the weirdest date she had ever been on.

Brian didn't even hear her angry sigh, though.

Bobby and Grizelda were heading into the haunted house. And she was still wearing that stupid T-shirt!

"Wait, I have a better idea," Brian yelped, pulling Rachel away from Bobby and Grizelda. "It's perfect for you. The Maze of Mirrors!"

"Okay," Rachel said. "Are you going to go in with me?"

"Of course," Brian assured her. *She'll never be able to tell if I'm really in there or not*, he thought. *That'll give me just enough time to go back and get Courtenay out of the Tunnel of Love!*

o o o

"Man, look at the cables on that thing," Joe said as he and Tommy gazed at the underside of one of the carnival rides.

"Yeah, it's an amazing piece of machinery," Tommy agreed. He was getting a little frustrated. Joe was a great guy, and he really knew his pistons. But he was supposed to be talking about Courtenay! So far he'd only said that Courtenay was mad, and that he was bummed about it. He seemed to think everything was hopeless between them.

"Hey, isn't that your girlfriend?" Tommy asked, pointing at Courtenay. Then he did a major double take. That guy holding her hand and dragging her over to the carousel—wasn't that Brian Keller?

Tommy squinted, trying to get a better look. The guy wouldn't turn around. But he was tall and blond, and he was wearing a denim jacket that looked exactly like Brian's. He gallantly selected a tall, black steed for Courtenay, then buckled her in carefully.

"I guess that's her date for the evening," Joe muttered, glaring at them.

Tommy was totally confused. What was Brian doing on a date with Courtenay? Wasn't he interested in Rachel? He shook his head. This was too much for him to figure out. Besides, he was supposed to be concentrating on Joe.

"Man, how can you let her go out with another guy?" Tommy asked, as they started walking again, making a large circle around the carousel.

"I don't know. It's kind of out of my control," Joe said. "I mean, things were great when we first met—before we were both famous. Now we have a lot more work—talk shows, modeling shoots, interviews. It's really crazy." He shook his head. "Maybe she didn't really like me that much in the first place. Maybe she was just going out with me because we were on the set together, and now that she's so busy, it's not going to work out for us." He sighed. "Maybe two people with our schedules just aren't meant to be together."

"So what are you going to do, go out with a girl that doesn't do anything but wait around for you?" Tommy kicked a little rock out of his path. "That's lame. If you love her, you should do everything you can to keep her."

"Well, what can I do? Look at her. She's having a great time!" Joe waved an arm at Courtenay, who was whizzing past them. The music was blaring and the lights were swishing around at a dizzying speed.

"By herself? On the merry-go-round?" Tommy shook his head. "Listen, man. I used to always think Lindsay would be better off without me. We almost broke up about a million times! But finally, one of my friends pointed out that she wouldn't go out with me if she didn't like me. You know?"

"It seems kind of obvious," Joe said.

"Well, it is. And it's true for Courtenay, too. I mean, the fact that you're both so busy can be a pain, but it means that everything's that much better when you do see each other. And you both have a lot more to talk about!"

"Huh," Joe grunted. "Well, she doesn't want to see me, anyway. She's out with that other guy."

"She's by herself now," Tommy pointed out. The

carousel was grinding to a halt, and Courtenay was looking around for Brian, who was nowhere to be found. She began fumbling with the buckle herself.

"Go on, man. Talk to her!" Tommy encouraged. Joe hesitated for half a second, then took off like a shot and appeared at Courtenay's side, helping her off her horse.

Tommy nodded, satisfied. He felt like he had just tuned up a Cadillac! But seeing Courtenay and Joe together again made him miss Lindsay. Where was she?

o o o

"Joe!" Courtenay exclaimed. She had been looking so hard for Brian that she hadn't even seen him standing right next to her. She slid off her horse and stood there, feeling a little embarrassed.

"Nice horse," he said. "Looks like Beauty."

"Good old Beauty. Your favorite girlfriend," Courtenay said, stepping off the carousel. It was an old joke between them. Joe had always said his car was the only woman that came between him and Courtenay.

"You're my girlfriend," Joe insisted. "At least, you used to be."

"Yeah." Courtenay's heart was in her throat. What

was Joe trying to say—that she wasn't his girlfriend anymore? "I used to be," she echoed.

Joe walked off the carousel, and Courtenay followed. "You look nice," he said.

"Thanks," she replied. They stood there awkwardly for a few more seconds.

"I've really . . . I mean . . ." Courtenay swallowed. "I miss you," she said.

Joe grimaced. "I miss you, too," he admitted.

"You do?" she asked, feeling relief wash over her.

Joe grinned. "Of course, silly," he said, reaching out to take her hand. "But that's not going to make our schedules easier to handle." He frowned. "And then there's the fact that you're on a date with some other guy," he added.

"It doesn't mean anything," Courtenay admitted. "I just agreed to go out with him because you flew off the handle when I had to get tutored the other day," she added.

"I'm sorry about that," Joe said turning to face her. "I was really a jerk. I had no right to tell you not to do stuff just because of me."

"Well, I should have been more understanding," Courtenay offered. "I mean, it's really nice to know that you want to hang out with me." She reached her arms around him and gave him a giant squeeze. "And I want to be with you, too! We'll just have to do our best to work around our schedules and make the most of the time we *do* spend together."

"Yeah; what's the point of even seeing each other if all we do is fight?" Joe leaned down and gave Courtenay a soft kiss that turned her knees to jelly. "It's a big waste of time. Let's not fight anymore. Deal?"

"Deal." Courtenay grinned at her boyfriend. Then she let out a little shriek.

"What?" Joe asked, alarmed.

"I'm supposed to be on a date with this guy Brian!" she said. "Now I'm going to have to blow him off."

"Why don't you just let me break both his legs?" Joe offered.

"Joe, you can't get mad at him," Courtenay chided. "He was just being nice."

"Humph," Joe grunted.

Just then, Megan, Dave, Lindsay, and Tommy came from the haunted house, laughing and making scary faces at one another.

"Hey, look, it's my new friends," Courtenay said. "I want you to meet them!" She made her way over to them, tugging on Joe's hand.

"Well, it looks like you guys have worked things out," Megan said a few minutes later, after everyone had been introduced. She was really psyched.

Courtenay had turned out to be a lot of fun, and now they were all hanging out together at the carnival!

"Hey, I know you," Joe said, squinting at Tommy. "Is that some sort of coincidence?"

"Sort of," Tommy admitted with a shrug. The two guys laughed and started talking about cars again, and Courtenay grabbed Megan and Lindsay and pulled them aside.

"You guys, I'm on a date with that guy I told you about, and I have to tell him that Joe and I are back together! I feel terrible."

"We'll figure something out." Lindsay squeezed her arm reassuringly. But there was no time to make plans, because Brian was coming around the corner!

Courtenay swallowed hard and stepped forward. She was just going to have to be brave and tell him the truth. "I'm really sorry, Brian," she said, staring at the ground. "But I'm going to have to break my date with you tonight."

"Date?" Courtenay heard a female voice say. "You were on a date with Brian?" Courtenay looked up. Rachel—the girl from the gab session in the *Beacon* offices—was standing right next to Brian. And he was holding her hand!

"Yeah, I was on a date with him tonight," Courtenay said. Now what was going on?

"*I* was on a date with Brian tonight," Rachel said. She stared at Courtenay, her eyes narrowing. Courtenay stared back. Then they both looked at Brian as an apprehensive hush fell over the gang.

"Where have you guys been?" Bobby's voice piped up, interrupting the showdown. Everyone turned to look at him and Grizelda.

"Hey, you know what's really funny?" Bobby went on, not noticing the tension. "Brian's in the background in the picture on Grizelda's shirt!"

All eyes swiveled down to the picture on the T-shirt. None of the gang had really looked at it before, but now everything was perfectly clear. The image of Brian being kissed by Courtenay said it all.

"That was the day after the balloons," Rachel said mournfully.

"You were hitting on her the day before you asked me out?" Courtenay asked indignantly.

Brian looked from one set of beautiful blue eyes to the other. He was completely, undeniably, indisputably busted.

But there was always the Keller charm—it might still work.

"Did I ever mention that in Switzerland, dating two girls at once is a time-honored tradition?"

"Still no sightings?" Megan asked as she slid into the booth at the Max.

"No Killer Keller." Bobby shook his head.

The Bayside gang—except for Brian—was sitting together in a booth. They had spent the morning looking for him, but he was totally missing in action.

"I can't believe he slipped away from us last night," Tommy said, thumping the table in annoyance. "I mean, he told that totally stupid story about double-dating in Switzerland, and the next thing you know—"

"El Disappearo," Lindsay sighed. "Like the Loch Ness monster."

"Like Elvis at a truck stop," Bobby added.

"Like Lindsay on Super Bowl Sunday," Tommy said.

"Like my life when I get my report card!" Rachel wailed. "Thanks to him, I didn't get any of my tutoring with Grizelda. The test is this afternoon. And I'm going to flunk it for sure!"

"Why so glum, chums?" Brian asked cheerfully as he appeared next to the table. Everyone stared at him for about five seconds, dumbfounded. Why was he so pleased with himself?

"Brian Keller, you are dead meat," Megan hissed.

"Worse than that. You're beef jerky!" Bobby added.

"If I were you, I wouldn't be looking so happy," Tommy said.

Brian held up his hands. "You have every right to be totally mad at me," he said. "But hear me out. I've got something to tell all of you."

The Bayside gang looked at one another, then back at Brian.

"Go ahead," Lindsay said.

"First of all, I'm really sorry." He sat down across from Rachel. "Especially to you. I got to this school, and you were my dream girl. I had to have a date with you!"

"Well, I can understand that," Rachel said, tossing her head defiantly. But she still looked furious.

112

"I just got starry-eyed with Courtenay," he went on. "But you're the one I really care about. And I took advantage of your boyfriend situation, just to get you to go out with me. That was wrong."

Rachel looked up sharply. "You bet it was," she snapped. "I can't believe I fell for all that!"

"My feelings were real," he said earnestly. "But I don't expect you to believe that."

"What about my test?" Rachel responded. "Are you going to explain all this to my parents?"

"No, I explained it to someone else," Brian said. He gestured to people at the door of the Max, and Ms. Fenster and Mr. Belding walked over.

"Brian told me about his little subterfuge," Ms. Fenster said primly, her lips pursed. "And while I disapprove of the fact that you allowed yourself to be distracted, I must say I was moved by his plea on your behalf."

"What Ms. Fenster is trying to say is, I approved a special extension in this case," Mr. Belding added. "Rachel, you have an extra week to study for the test."

Rachel's jaw dropped. "Thank you," was all she could think of to say. "I promise, I'll study till my false eyelashes fall off!"

"Just do well on the test." Mr. Belding grimaced. Then he and Ms. Fenster turned and left.

"Well, thank you," Rachel said grudgingly to Brian.

"Now do you believe that I'm really sorry?" he asked anxiously.

"I believe you. But I'm still mad," Rachel replied.

"That was really nice of you," Lindsay added. "But you can't play with people's feelings!"

As if on cue, the door to the Max opened and in walked the most famous teen couple in Hollywood. As usual, the whole room got quiet.

Courtenay and Joe scanned the room anxiously, searching for their new friends. When Megan waved, Courtenay smiled and they walked over. But Joe looked as if he wanted to wring Brian's neck.

"There's one more person you need to apologize to," Lindsay said pointedly.

As if Brian didn't know that! The problem was, he didn't know how to start. As Courtenay and Joe approached the table, he took a deep breath. But before he could say anything, Courtenay started talking.

"Brian, you totally took advantage of me," she said. "You used my vulnerability from my fight with Joe to get me to go on a date with you. You were completely dishonest."

"You're right," Brian admitted. "I was really wrong and I'm sorry. Is there any way I can make it up to you?"

"Oh, I don't know," Courtenay said, smiling slyly. "What are you willing to do?"

"Anything," Brian offered.

"Absolutely anything?" Joe countered.

"I promise, I'll do absolutely anything," Brian answered. But he had the sneaking suspicion that he was agreeing to something he was going to regret. . . .

chapter

A week later, the whole school was assembled in the Bayside auditorium. Mr. Belding was trying to quiet everyone, but there was a buzz of excitement in the air.

"Please, students!" Mr. Belding begged. "I need your attention. Okay? Hello!" The rumble of students was still too loud.

Then Vice Principal Screech appeared from the wings of the stage. He cleared his throat a few times into the microphone. Then he stuck his fingers into his mouth and let out a piercing whistle. "*Tu-wheeeeet!*" It echoed off all the walls, and the room was instantly silent. Screech shrugged and walked off the stage.

"Thank you," Mr. Belding said. "Now I know you're all terribly excited about seeing the *LoveSchool* scenes that were filmed here at Bayside. We're very excited that the producers offered this special sneak preview!"

Everyone clapped and cheered.

"All right, then. Without further ado, I offer you a sneak preview of some *LoveSchool* movie scenes!" The lights went down and the scenes began.

Everyone laughed at the sight of Mr. Belding saying a few lines, looking stiff and uncomfortable. And little groups squealed and pointed when they recognized themselves or their friends in the background of the scenes. But Rachel, Lindsay, and Megan knew that the best part was being saved for last.

"You guys, this has gone far enough," the on-screen Courtenay was saying. "Somebody has been scheming and planning, trying to manipulate us into hating each other."

"I know," Joe's character responded. "I just wish I knew who. I'd love to get my hands on whoever it was!"

"Well, you're going to get your chance," Courtenay said triumphantly. "I figured out that the person who's been causing all this trouble is that creepy little nerd!"

The *LoveSchool* kids put their heads together to come up with a plan, and the screen faded to black.

In the next scene, a total geekoid entered the picture. He was wearing plaid polyester pants that barely came down to his ankles, doofy dress loafers, and an Urkel T-shirt. He had thick, heavy glasses, and his hair was blow-dried till it was puffy and totally weird-looking.

"Wow, what a stud!" Grizelda and one of her friends gasped. "Who is that guy?"

"Take this, you geeky creep!" Courtenay squealed. She and the rest of the cast attacked the nerd with ketchup, mustard, and Silly String. Then Joe dropped a bucket of water on his head. As the slimy mess dripped off the nerd, he looked directly at the camera and whined, "It's not faaaaiiiirrrr!"

The auditorium erupted in laughter as everyone recognized their resident I'm-so-cool guy. It was Brian Keller!

"It's not faaaaiiiirrrr," a couple of girls a few rows back whined, imitating him.

"Hey, Keller, is everything faaaaiiiirrrr?" one of the football players laughed, punching him in the arm as he tried to slink down in his seat. "Come on, say it!" the football player encouraged him. "*Say it!*"

"It's not faaaaiiiirrrr," Brian whined halfheartedly, as the football guys joined the rest of the school in laughing at him. He could see it now: The annoying phrase was going to follow him throughout his high school career!

"Gosh, Brian," Rachel said, grinning and leaning across the rest of the gang to talk to him. "I didn't realize what a natural you are. You make a great geek!"

When the gang gets the chance to represent Bayside on a TV game show, they're totally psyched! But it's not long before things get out of control. Rachel develops a mad crush on the show's host. Megan gets out-of-control bossy. And Brian is working so hard at his new job that he falls asleep during the finals!

Will the gang survive "Smarts and Strength"? Find out when you read

May the Best Team Win,

the exciting new novel about Bayside's new class!